Marx
Defoe Abbott Hardy Montaigne Machiavelli Chesterton Cooper Emerson Joyce Austen
Melville Haggard Hugo Grimm
Stoker Carroll Christie Molière Eliot
Wilde Maupassant Byron Schiller
Garnett Einstein Fitzgerald Engels Smith Kafka
Goethe Hawthorne Kipling Doyle Hall
Cotton Dostoyevsky Willis
Baum Henry Nietzsche Balzac
Leslie Dumas Flaubert Turgenev Crane
Stockton Vatsyayana Verne
Burroughs Whitman Gogol Vinci
Curtis Tocqueville Busch
Homer Widger Tolstoy
Darwin Thoreau Twain Scott
Potter Freud Zola Lawrence Plato Harte
Kant Jowett Stevenson Dickens Hesse
Andersen Cervantes Burton
London Descartes Voltaire
Poe Aristotle Wells Cooke
Hale James Hastings
Bunner Shakespeare Irving
Richter Chambers
Doré da Shaw Benedict Alcott
Dante Chekhov Pushkin
Swift Wodehouse Newton

Norse Tales and Sketches

Alexander Lange Kielland

Imprint

This book is part of TREDITION CLASSICS

Author: Alexander Lange Kielland
Cover design: Buchgut, Berlin – Germany

Publisher: tredition GmbH, Hamburg - Germany
ISBN: 978-3-8424-7625-7

www.tredition.com
www.tredition.de

Copyright:
The content of this book is sourced from the public domain.

The intention of the TREDITION CLASSICS series is to make world literature in the public domain available in printed format. Literary enthusiasts and organizations, such as Project Gutenberg, worldwide have scanned and digitally edited the original texts. tredition has subsequently formatted and redesigned the content into a modern reading layout. Therefore, we cannot guarantee the exact reproduction of the original format of a particular historic edition. Please also note that no modifications have been made to the spelling, therefore it may differ from the orthography used today.

NORSE TALES AND SKETCHES.

BY

ALEXANDER L. KIELLAND.

TRANSLATED BY R. L. CASSIE.

INTRODUCTION

Encouraged by the great and growing popularity of Scandinavian literature in this country, I venture to submit to public judgment this humble essay towards an English presentment of some of the charming novelettes of Alexander L. Kielland, a writer who takes rank among the foremost exponents of modern Norse thought. Although these short stories do not represent the full fruition of the author's genius, they yet convey a fairly accurate conception of his literary personality, and of the bold realistic tendency which is so strikingly developed in his longer novels.

Kielland's style is polished, lucid, and incisive. He does not waste words or revel in bombastic diffuseness. Every phrase of his narrative is a definite contribution towards the vivification of his realistic effects. His concise, laconic periods are pregnant with deep meaning, and instinct with that indefinable Norse essence which almost eludes the translator—that vague something which specially lends itself to the treatment of weird or pathetic situations.

In his pre-eminence as a satirist, Kielland resembles Thackeray. His satire, although keen, is always wholesome, genial, and good-humoured.

Kielland's longer novels are masterly delineations of Norwegian provincial life and character, and his vivid individualization of his native town of Stavanger finds few parallels in fiction.

In conclusion, the writer hopes that this modest publication may help to draw the attention of the cultured British public to another of the great literary figures of the North.

R.L.C.

CONTENTS.

A SIESTA.

In an elegant suite of chambers in the Rue Castiglione sat a merry party at dessert.

Senhor José Francisco de Silvis was a short-legged, dark-complexioned Portuguese, one of those who usually come from Brazil with incredible wealth, live incredible lives in Paris, and, above all, become notorious by making the most incredible acquaintances.

In that little company scarcely anybody, except those who had come in pairs, knew his neighbour. And the host himself knew his guests only through casual meetings at balls, *tables d' hôte*, or in the street.

Senhor de Silvis laughed much, and talked loudly of his success in life, as is the habit of rich foreigners; and as he could not reach up to the level of the Jockey Club, he gathered the best company he could find. When he met anyone, he immediately asked for the address, and sent next day an invitation to a little dinner. He spoke all languages, even German, and one could see by his face that he was not a little proud when he called over the table: Mein lieber Herr Doctor! Wie geht's Ihnen?'

There was actually a live German doctor among this merry party. He had an overgrown light-red beard, and that Sedan smile which invariably accompanies the Germans in Paris.

The temperature of the conversation rose with the champagne; the sounds of fluent and broken French were mingled with those of Spanish and Portuguese. The ladies lay back in their chairs and laughed. The guests already knew each other well enough not to be reserved or constrained. Jokes and *bons-mots* passed over the table, and from mouth to mouth. 'Der liebe Doctor' alone engaged in a serious discussion with the gentleman next to him—a French journalist with a red ribbon in his buttonhole.

And there was one more who was not drawn into the general merriment. He sat on the right of Mademoiselle Adèle, while on the left was her new lover, the corpulent Anatole, who had surfeited himself on truffles.

During dinner Mademoiselle Adèle had endeavoured, by many innocent little arts, to infuse some life into her right-hand neighbour. However, he remained very quiet, answering her courteously, but briefly, and in an undertone.

At first she thought he was a Pole—one of those very tiresome specimens who wander about and pretend to be outlaws. However, she soon perceived that she had made a mistake, and this piqued Mademoiselle Adèle. For one of her many specialties was the ability to immediately 'assort' all the foreigners with whom she mingled, and she used to declare that she could guess a man's nationality as soon as she had spoken ten words with him.

But this taciturn stranger caused her much perplexed cogitation. If he had only been fair-haired, she would at once have set him down as an Englishman, for he talked like one. But he had dark hair, a thick black moustache, and a nice little figure. His fingers were remarkably long, and he had a peculiar way of trifling with his bread and playing with his dessert-fork.

'He is a musician,' whispered Mademoiselle Adèle to her stout friend.

'Ah!' replied Monsieur Anatole. 'I am afraid I have eaten too many truffles.'

Mademoiselle Adèle whispered in his ear some words of good counsel, upon which he laughed and looked very affectionate.

However, she could not relinquish her hold of the interesting foreigner. After she had coaxed him to drink several glasses of champagne, he became livelier, and talked more.

'Ah!' cried she suddenly; 'I hear it in your speech. You are an Englishman!'

The stranger grew quite red in the face, and answered quickly, 'No, madame.'

Mademoiselle Adèle laughed. 'I beg your pardon. I know that Americans feel angry when they are taken for Englishmen.'

'Neither am I an American,' replied the stranger.

This was too much for Mademoiselle Adèle. She bent over her plate and looked sulky, for she saw that Mademoiselle Louison opposite was enjoying her defeat.

The foreign gentleman understood the situation, and added, half aloud: 'I am an Irishman, madame.'

'Ah!' said Mademoiselle Adèle, with a grateful smile, for she was easily reconciled.

'Anatole! Irishman—what is that?' she asked in a whisper.

'The poor of England,' he whispered back.

'Indeed!'

Adèle elevated her eyebrows, and cast a shrinking, timid glance at the stranger. She had suddenly lost much of her interest in him.

De Silvis's dinners were excellent. The party had sat long at table, and when Monsieur Anatole thought of the oysters with which the feast had begun, they appeared to him like a beautiful dream. On the contrary, he had a somewhat too lively recollection of the truffles.

Dinner was over; hands were reaching out for glasses, or trifling with fruit or biscuits.

That sentimental blonde, Mademoiselle Louison, fell into meditation over a grape that she had dropped in her champagne glass. Tiny bright air-bubbles gathered all round the coating of the fruit, and when it was quite covered with these shining white pearls, they lifted the heavy grape up through the wine to the surface.

'Look!' said Mademoiselle Louison, turning her large, swimming eyes upon the journalist, 'look, white angels are bearing a sinner to heaven!'

'Ah! *charmant*, mademoiselle! What a sublime thought!' exclaimed the journalist, enraptured.

Mademoiselle Louison's sublime thought passed round the table, and was much admired. Only the frivolous Adèle whispered to her obese admirer, 'It would take a good many angels to bear you, Anatole.'

Meanwhile the journalist seized the opportunity; he knew how to rivet the general attention. Besides, he was glad to escape from a tiresome political controversy with the German; and, as he wore a red ribbon and affected the superior journalistic tone, everybody listened to him.

He explained how small forces, when united, can lift great burdens; and then he entered upon the topic of the day—the magnificent collections made by the press for the sufferers by the floods in Spain, and for the poor of Paris. Concerning this he had much to relate, and every moment he said 'we,' alluding to the press. He talked himself quite warm about 'these millions, that we, with such great self-sacrifice, have raised.'

But each of the others had his own story to tell. Numberless little touches of nobility—all savouring of self-denial—came to light from amidst these days of luxury and pleasure.

Mademoiselle Louison's best friend—an insignificant little lady who sat at the foot of the table—told, in spite, of Louison's protest, how the latter had taken three poor seamstresses up to her own rooms, and had them sew the whole of the night before the *fête* in the hippodrome. She had given the poor girls coffee and food, besides payment.

Mademoiselle Louison suddenly became an important personage at table, and the journalist began to show her marked attention.

The many pretty instances of philanthropy, and Louison's swimming eyes, put the whole company into a quiet, tranquil, benevolent frame of mind, eminently in keeping with the weariness induced by the exertions of the feast. And this comfortable feeling rose yet a few degrees higher after the guests were settled in soft easy-chairs in the cool drawing-room.

There was no other light than the fire in the grate. Its red glimmer crept over the English carpet and up the gold borders in the tapestry; it shone upon a gilt picture-frame, on the piano that stood opposite, and, here and there, on a face further away in the gloom.

Nothing else was visible except the red ends of cigars and cigarettes.

The conversation died away. The silence was broken only by an occasional whisper or the sound of a coffee-cup being put aside; each seemed disposed to enjoy, undisturbed, his genial mood and the quiet gladness of digestion. Even Monsieur Anatole forgot his truffles, as he reclined in a low chair close to the sofa, on which Mademoiselle Adèle had taken her seat.

'Is there no one who will give us a little music?' asked Senhor de Silvis from his chair. 'You are always so kind, Mademoiselle Adèle.'

'Oh no, no!' cried Mademoiselle; 'I am too tired.'

But the foreigner—the Irishman—rose from his corner and walked towards the instrument.

'Ah, you will play for us! A thousand thanks, Monsieur——.' Senhor de Silvis had forgotten the name—a thing that often happened to him with his guests.

'He is a musician,' said Mademoiselle Adèle to her friend. Anatole grunted admiringly.

Indeed, all were similarly impressed by the mere way in which he sat down and, without any preparation, struck a few chords here and there, as if to wake the instrument.

Then he began to play—lightly, sportively, frivolously, as befitted the situation. The melodies of the day were intermingled with fragments of waltzes and ballads; all the ephemeral trifles that Paris hums over for eight days he blended together with brilliantly fluent execution.

The ladies uttered exclamations of admiration, and sang a few bars, keeping time with their feet. The whole party followed the music with intense interest; the strange artist had hit their mood, and drawn them all with him from the beginning. 'Der liebe Doctor' alone listened with the Sedan smile on his face; the pieces were too easy for him.

But soon there came something for the German too; he nodded now and then with a sort of appreciation.

It was a strange situation: the piquant fragrance that filled the air, the pleasure-loving women — these people, so free and unconstrained, all strangers to one another, hidden in the elegant, half-dark salon, each following his most secret thoughts — thoughts born of the mysterious, muffled music; whilst the firelight rose and fell, and made everything that was golden glimmer in the darkness.

And there constantly came more for the doctor. From time to time he turned and signed to De Silvis, as he heard the loved notes of 'unser Schumann,' 'unser Beethoven,' or even of 'unser famoser Richard.'

Meanwhile the stranger played on, steadily and without apparent effort, slightly inclined to the left, so as to give power to the bass. It sounded as if he had twenty fingers, all of steel; he knew how to unite the multitudinous notes in a single powerful clang. Without any pause to mark the transition from one melody to another, he riveted the interest of the company by constant new surprises, graceful allusions, and genial combinations, so that even the least musical among them were constrained to listen with eager attention.

But the character of the music imperceptibly changed. The artist bent constantly over the instrument, inclining more to the left, and there was a strange unrest in the bass notes. The Baptists from 'The Prophet' came with heavy step; a rider from 'Damnation de Faust' dashed up from far below, in a desperate, hobbling hell-gallop.

The rumbling grew stronger and stronger down in the depths, and Monsieur Anatole again began to feel the effects of the truffles. Mademoiselle Adèle half rose; the music would not let her lie in peace.

Here and there the firelight shone on a pair of black eyes staring at the artist. He had lured them with him, and now they could not break loose; downward, ever downward, he led them — downward, where was a dull and muffled murmur as of threatenings and plaints.

'Er führt eine famose linke Hand,' said the doctor. But De Silvis did not hear him; he sat, like the others, in breathless expectancy.

A dark, sickening dread went out from the music and spread itself over them all. The artist's left hand seemed to be tying a knot that would never be loosened, while his right made light little runs, like flames, up and down in the treble. It sounded as if there was something uncanny brewing down in the cellar, whilst those above burnt torches and made merry.

A sigh was heard, a half-scream from one of the ladies, who felt ill; but no one heeded it. The artist had now got quite down into the bass, and his tireless fingers whirled the notes together, so that a cold shudder crept down the backs of all.

But into that threatening, growling sound far below there began to come an upward movement. The notes ran into, over, past each other—upward, always upward, but without making any way. There was a wild struggle to get up, as it were a multitude of small, dark figures scratching and tearing; a mad eagerness, a feverish haste; a scrambling, a seizing with hands and teeth; kicks, curses, shrieks, prayers—and all the while the artist's hands glided upward so slowly, so painfully slowly.

'Anatole,' whispered Adèle, pale as death, 'he is playing Poverty.'

'Oh, these truffles!' groaned Anatole, holding his stomach.

All at once the room was lit up. Two servants with lamps and candelabra appeared in the *portière*; and at the same moment the stranger finished by bringing down his fingers of steel with all his might in a dissonance, so startling, so unearthly, that the whole party sprang up.

'Out with the lamps!' shouted De Silvis.

'No, no!' shrieked Adèle; 'I dare not be in the dark. Oh, that dreadful man!'

Who was it? Yes, who was it? They involuntarily crowded round the host, and no one noticed the stranger slip out behind the servants.

De Silvis tried to laugh. 'I think it was the devil himself. Come, let us go to the opera.'

'To the opera! Not at any price!' exclaimed Louison. 'I will hear no music for a fortnight.'

'Oh, those truffles!' moaned Anatole.

The party broke up. They had all suddenly realized that they were strangers in a strange place, and each one wished to slip quietly home.

As the journalist conducted Mademoiselle Louison to her carriage, he said: 'Yes, this is the consequence of letting one's self be persuaded to dine with these semi-savages. One is never sure of the company he will meet.'

'Ah, how true! He quite spoiled my good spirits,' said Louison mournfully, turning her swimming eyes upon her companion. 'Will you accompany me to La Trinité? There is a low mass at twelve o'clock.'

The journalist bowed, and got into the carriage with her.

But as Mademoiselle Adèle and Monsieur Anatole drove past the English dispensary in the Rue de la Paix, he stopped the driver, and said pleadingly to his fair companion: 'I really think I must get out and get something for those truffles. You will excuse me, won't you? That music, you know.'

'Don't mind me, my friend. Speaking candidly, I don't think either of us is specially lively this evening. Good-night.'

She leant back in the carriage, relieved at finding herself alone; and this light, frivolous creature cried as if she had been whipped whilst she drove homeward.

Anatole was undoubtedly suffering from the truffles, but yet he thought he came to himself as the carriage rolled away. Never in their whole acquaintance had they been so well pleased with each other as at this moment of parting.

'Der liebe Doctor' had come best through the experience, because, being a German, he was hardened in music. All the same, he resolved to take a walk as far as Müller's *brasserie* in the Rue Richelieu to get a decent glass of German beer, and perhaps a little bacon, on the top of it all.

A MONKEY.

Yes, it was really a monkey that had nearly procured me 'Lauda-bilis' [Footnote: A second-class pass.] in my final law examination. As it was, I only got 'Haud'; [Footnote: A third-class pass.] but, after all, this was pretty creditable.

But my friend the advocate, who had daily, with mingled feelings, to read the drafts of my work, found my process-paper so good that he hoped it might raise me into the 'Laud' list. And he did not wish me to suffer the injury and annoyance of being plucked in the *vivâ voce* examination, for he knew me and was my friend.

But the monkey was really a coffee-stain on the margin of page 496 of Schweigaard's Process, which I had borrowed from my friend Cucumis.

Going up to a law examination in slush and semi-darkness in mid-winter is one of the saddest experiences that a man can have. It may, indeed, be even worse in summer; but this I have not tried.

One rushes through these eleven papers (or is it thirteen? — it is certainly the most infamous number that the college authorities have been able to devise) — like an unhappy *débutant* in a circus. He stands on the back of a galloping horse, with his life in his hands and a silly circus smile on his lips; and so he must leap eleven (or is it thirteen?) times through one of these confounded paper-covered hoops.

The unhappy mortal who passes — or tries to pass — his law examination, finds himself in precisely the same situation, only he does not gallop round a ring, under brilliant gaslight, to the music of a full band. He sits upon a hard chair in semi-darkness with his face to the wall, and the only sound he hears is the creaking of the inspectors' boots. For in all the wide, wide world there are no such creaky boots as those of law examination inspectors.

And so comes the dreadful moment when the black-robed tormentor from the Collegium Juridicum brings in the examination-paper. He plants himself in the doorway, and reads. Coldly, impassively, with a cruel mockery of the horror of the situation, he raises aloft this fateful document—this wretched paper-covered hoop, through which we must all spring, or dismount and wend our way back—on foot!

The candidates settle themselves in the saddle. Some seem quite unable to get firmly seated; they rock uneasily hither and thither, and one rider dismounts. He is followed to the door by all eyes, and a sigh runs through the assembled students. 'You to-day; I to-morrow.'

Meanwhile one begins to hear a light trotting over the paper; they are leaping.

Some few individuals sit firmly and gracefully through it all, and come out on the other side 'standing for Laud.' Others think that leaping straight is too easy; therefore, they turn in the air and alight with backs first. These also get through, but backwards; and it is said that their agility does not win from the judges its deserved meed of appreciation.

Again, others leap, but miss the hoop. They spring underneath, to one side—some even high over the top, alighting safe and sound on the other side. These latter generally find the paper extremely simple, and continue the wild ride quite unconcernedly.

But if one is not fond of riding, and has had no practice in leaping, he is much to be pitied—unless, indeed, he has a monkey on page 496.

I do not know how many hoops I had passed when I found myself face to face with the process-paper.

It was an unhealthy life that we then led: leaping by day and reading by night. I sat at midnight half-way through Schweigaard's Process, alternately putting my head out of the window and into the washhand basin, and, between whiles, rushing like a whirlwind through the withered leaves of the musty volume.

However, even the most violent wind must eventually fall; and, indeed, this was my heartfelt wish. But the juridical momentum was strong within me. I sat stiffly, peering and reading for the eleventh time: 'One might thus certainly assume'—'One—might—thus—certainly,'— combine the useful with the agreeable—and lean back—a little in the chair. I can read just as well; the lamp doesn't bother me in the least. 'One—might—thus—'

But all manner of non-juridical images rose up from the book, entwined themselves about the lamp, and threatened to completely overshadow my clear legal brain. I could yet dimly see the white paper. 'One—might— thus—'. The rest disappeared in a myriad of small dark characters that flowed down the closely-printed pages; in dull despair my eyes followed the stream, and then I saw, towards the bottom of the right-hand page, a face.

It was a monkey that was drawn on the margin. It was excellently drawn, I thought, the brown colouring of the face being especially remarkable. I am ashamed to say that my interest in this work of art proved stronger than Schweigaard himself. I roused myself a little, and leant forward in order to see better.

By turning the leaf, I discovered that the remarkable brown colouring of the face was due to the fact that the whole monkey, after all, was only a coffee-stain. The artist had merely added a pair of eyes and a little hair; the genial expression of the picture was really to be credited to the individual who had spilt the coffee.

'Cucumis couldn't draw,' thought I; that I knew. 'But, by Jove! he *could* do his process!'

And now I came to think of Cucumis, of his handsome degree, of his triumphant home-coming, and of how much he must have read in order to become so learned. And, while I thought of all this, my consciousness awoke little by little, until my own ignorance suddenly stood clearly before me in all its horrible nakedness.

I pictured to myself the shame of having to 'dismount,' or, still worse, of being that one unfortunate of whom it is invariably said with sinister anonymity, 'One of the candidates received *non contemnendus*'. And as it sometimes happens that people lose their reason through much learning, so I grew half crazy with terror at my ignorance.

Up I jumped, and dipped my head in the wash-basin. Scarcely taking time to dry myself, I began to read with an energy that fixed every word in my memory.

Down the left page I hurried, with unabated vigour down the right; I reached the monkey, rushed past him, turned the leaf, and read bravely on.

I was not conscious of the fact that my strength was now completely exhausted. Although I caught a glimpse of a new section (usually so strong an incentive to increased effort), I could not help getting entangled in one of those artful propositions that one reads over and over again in illusory profundity.

I groped about for a way of escape, but there was none. Incoherent thoughts began to whirl through my brain. 'Where is the monkey?—a spot of coffee—one cannot be genial on both sides—everything in life has a right and a wrong side—for example, the university clock—but if I cannot swim, let me come out—I am going to the circus—I know very well that you are standing there grinning at me, Cucumis—but I can leap through the hoop, I can—and if that professor who is standing smoking at my paraffin lamp had only conscientiously referred to *corpus juris*, I should not now be lying here—in my night-shirt in the middle of Karl Johan's Gade [Footnote: A principal street of Christiania.]—but—' Then I sank into that deep, dreamless slumber which only falls to the lot of an evil conscience when one is very young.

I was in the saddle early next morning.

I don't know if the devil ever had shoes on, but I must suppose he had, for his inspectors were in their boots, and they creaked past me, where I sat in my misery with my face to the wall.

A professor walked round the rooms and looked at the victims. Occasionally he nodded and smiled encouragingly, as his eye fell on one of those miserable lick-spittles who frequent the lectures; but when he discovered me, the smile vanished, and his ice-cold stare seemed to write upon the wall over my head: 'Mene, mene! [Footnote: Dan. v. 25.] Wretch, I know thee not!'

A pair of inspectors walked creakily up to the professor and fawned upon him; I heard them whispering behind my chair. I ground my teeth in silent wrath at the thought that these contemptible creatures were paid for—yes, actually made their living by torturing me and some of my best friends.

The door opened; a glimmering yellow light fell upon the white faces; it called to mind 'The Victims of Terrorism' in Luxembourg. Then all again became dark, and the black-robed emissary of the College flitted through the room like a bat, with the famous white document in his claws.

He began to read.

Never in my life had I been less inclined for leaping; and yet I started violently at the first words. 'The monkey!' I had almost shouted; for he it was—it was evidently the coffee-stain on page 496. The paper bore precisely upon what I had read with so much energy the preceding night.

And I began to write. After a short, but superior and assured preamble, I introduced the high-sounding words of Schweigaard, 'One might thus certainly assume,' etc., and hurried down the left page, with unabated vigour down the right, reached the monkey, dashed past him, began to grope and fumble, and then I found I could not write a word more.

I felt that something was wanting, but I knew that it was useless to speculate; what a man can't do, he can't. I therefore made a full stop, and went away long before any of the others were half finished.

He has dismounted, thought my fellow-sufferers, or he may have leaped wide of the hoop. For it was a difficult paper.

'Why,' said the advocate, as he read, 'you are better than I thought. This is pure Schweigaard. You have left out the last point, but that doesn't matter very much; one can see that you are well up in these things. But why, then, were you so pitiably afraid of the process yesterday?'

'I didn't know a thing.'

He laughed. 'Was it last night, then, that you learned your process?'

'Yes.'

'Did anyone help you?'

'Yes.'

'He must be a devil of a crammer who could put so much law into your head in one night. May I ask what wizard it was?'

'A monkey!' I replied.

A TALE OF THE SEA.

Once there lay in a certain haven a large number of vessels. They had lain there very long, not exactly on account of storm, but rather because of a dead calm; and at last they had lain there until they no longer heeded the weather.

All the captains had gradually become good friends; they visited from ship to ship, and called one another 'Cousin.'

They were in no hurry to depart. Now and then a youthful steersman might chance to let fall a word about a good wind and a smooth sea. But such remarks were not tolerated; order had to be maintained on a ship. Those, therefore, who could not hold their tongues were set ashore.

Matters could not, however, go on thus for ever. Men are not so good as they ought to be, and all do not thrive under law and order.

The crews at length began to murmur a little; they were weary of painting and polishing the cabins, and of rowing the captains to and from the toddy suppers. It was rumoured that individual ships were getting ready for sailing. The sails of some were set one by one in all silence, the anchors were weighed without song, and the ships glided quietly out of the harbour; others sailed while their captains slept. Fighting and mutiny were also heard of; but then there came help from the neighbour captains, the malcontents were punished and put ashore, and all moorings were carefully examined and strengthened.

Nevertheless, all the ships, except one, at last left the harbour. They did not all sail with like fortune; one and another even came in again for a time, damaged. Others were little heard of. The captain of one ship, it was said, was thrown overboard by his men; another sailed with half the crew in irons, none knew where. But yet they were all in motion, each striving after its own fashion, now in storm, now in calm, towards its goal.

As stated, only one ship remained in the harbour, and it lay safe and sound, with two anchors at the bottom and three great cables attached to the quay.

It was a strange little craft. The hull was old, but it had been newly repaired, and they had given it a smart little modern figurehead, which contrasted strangely with the smooth sides and the heavy stern. One could see that the rigging had originally belonged to a large vessel, but had been very hastily adapted to the smaller hull, and this still further increased the want of proportion in the brig's whole appearance. Then it was painted with large portholes for guns, like a man-of-war, and always carried its flag at the mainmast.

The skipper was no common man. He himself had painted the sketch of the brig that hung in the cabin, and, besides, he could sing — both psalms and songs. Indeed, there were those who maintained that he composed the songs himself; but this was most probably a lie. And it was certainly a lie that they whispered in the forecastle: that the skipper had not quite got his sea-legs. Young men always tell such stories to cabin-boys, in order to appear manly. And, besides, there was a steersman on the brig, who could, on a pinch, easily round the headlands alone.

He had sailed as steersman for many years of our Lord, ever since the time of the skipper's late father. He had become as if glued to the tiller, and many could scarcely imagine the old brig with a new steersman.

He had certainly never voyaged in distant waters; but as his trade had always been the same, and as he had invariably been in the company of others, the brig had sailed pretty fortunately, without special damage and without special merit.

Therefore, both he and the skipper had arrived at the conviction that none could sail better than they, and hence they cared little what the others did. They looked up at the sky and shook their heads.

The men felt quite comfortable, for they were not used to better things. Most of them could not understand why the crews of the other ships were in such a hurry to be off; the month went round all the same, whether one lay in port or sailed, and then it was better to avoid work. So long as the skipper made no sign of preparation for sailing, the men might keep their minds easy, for he must surely have the most interest in getting away. And besides, they all knew what sort of fellow the steersman was, and if such a capable and experienced man lay still, they might be quite sure that he had good and powerful reasons.

But a little party among the crew — some quite youthful persons — thought it was a shame to let themselves be thus left astern by everybody. They had, indeed, no special advantage or profit to expect from the voyage, but at last the inaction became intolerable, and they conceived the daring resolve of sending a youth aft to beg the captain to fix a date for sailing.

The more judicious among the crew crossed themselves, and humbly entreated the young man to keep quiet; but the latter was a rash greenhorn, who had sailed in foreign service, and therefore imagined himself to be a 'regular devil of a fellow.' He went right aft and down into the cabin, where the skipper and the steersman sat with their whisky before them, playing cards.

'We would ask if the skipper would kindly set sail next week, for now we are all so weary of lying here,' said the young man, looking the skipper straight in the eyes without winking.

The latter's face first turned pale blue, and then assumed a deep violet tint; but he restrained himself, and said, as was his invariable custom:

'What think you, steersman?'

'H'm,' replied the steersman slowly. More he never used to say at first, when he was questioned, for he did not like to answer promptly. But when he got an opportunity of speaking alone, without being interrupted, he could utter the longest sentences and the very hardest words. And then the skipper was especially proud of him.

However short the steersman's reply might seem, the skipper at once understood its meaning. He turned towards the youth—gravely, but gracefully, for he was an exceedingly well-bred man.

'You cursed young fool! don't you think I understand these things better than you? I, who have thought of nothing but being a skipper since I was knee-high! But I know well enough what you and the like of you are thinking about. You don't care a d— — about the craft, and if you could only get the power from us old ones, you would run her on the first islet you came to, so that you might plunder her of the whisky. But there will be none of that, my young whelp! Here we shall lie, as long as I choose.'

When this decision reached the forecastle, it awoke great indignation among the young and immature, which, indeed, was only to be expected. But even the skipper's friends and admirers shook their heads, and opined that it was a nasty answer; after all, it was only a civil question, which ought not to compromise anybody.

There now arose a growing ill-humour—something quite unheard-of among these peaceable fellows. Even the skipper, who was not usually quick to understand or remark anything, thought he saw many sullen faces, and he was no longer so well pleased with the bearing of the crew when he stepped out upon deck with his genial 'Good-morning, you rogues.'

But the steersman had long scented something, for he had a fine nose and long ears. Therefore, a couple of evenings after the young man's unfortunate visit, it was remarked that something extraordinary was brewing aft.

The cabin-boy had to make three journeys with the toddy-kettle, and the report he gave in the forecastle after his last trip was indeed disquieting.

The steersman seemed to have talked without intermission for two hours; before them on the table lay barometer, chronometer, sextant, journal, and half the ship's library. This consisted of Kingo's hymn-book and an old Dutch 'Kaart-Boikje';[Footnote: Chart-book.] for the skipper could do just as little with the new hymns as the steersman with the new charts.

The skipper now sat prodding the chart with a large pair of compasses, while the steersman talked, using all his longest and hardest words. There was one word in particular that was often repeated, and this the boy learned by heart. He said it over and over again to himself as he went up the cabin stairs and passed along the deck to the forecastle, and the moment he opened the door he shouted:

'Initiative! Mind that word, boys! Write it down—initiative!'

In-i-ti-a-tive was with much difficulty spelt out and written with chalk on the table. And during the boy's long statement all these men sat staring, uneasily and with anxious expectancy, at this long, mystic word.

'And then,' concluded the cabin-boy at last—'then says the steersman: "But we ourselves shall take the—" what is written on the table.'

All exclaimed simultaneously, 'Initiative.'

'Yes, that was it. And every time he said it, they both struck the table and looked at me as if they would eat me. I now think, therefore, that it is a new kind of revolver they intend to use upon us.'

But none of the others thought so; it was surely not so bad as that. But something was impending, that was clear. And the relieved watchman went to his berth with gloomy forebodings, and the middle watch did not get a wink of sleep that night.

At seven o'clock next morning both skipper and steersman were up on deck. No man could remember ever having seen them before so early in the day. But there was no time to stand in amazement, for now followed, in quick succession, orders for sailing.

'Heave up the anchors! Let two men go ashore and slip the cables!'

There was gladness and bustle among the crew, and the preparations proceeded so rapidly that in less than an hour the brig was under canvas.

The skipper looked at the steersman and shook his head, muttering, 'This is the devil's own haste.'

After a few little turns in the spacious harbour, the brig passed the headland and stood out to sea. A fresh breeze was blowing, and the waves ran rather high.

The steersman, with a prodigious twist in his mouth, stood astride the tiller, for such a piece of devil's trumpery as a wheel should never come on board as long as *he* had anything to say in the matter.

The skipper stood on the cabin stairs, with his head above the companion. His face was of a somewhat greenish hue, and he frequently ran down into the cabin. The old boatswain believed that he went to look at the chart, the young man thought he drank whisky, but the cabin-boy swore that he went below to vomit.

The men were in excellent spirits; it was so refreshing to breathe the sea air, and to feel the ship once again moving under their feet. Indeed, the old brig herself seemed to be in a good humour; she dived as deep down between the seas as she could, and raised much more foam than was necessary.

The young sailors looked out for heavy seas. 'Here comes a whopper,' they shouted; 'if it would only hit us straight!' And it did.

It was a substantial sea, larger than the others. It approached deliberately, and seemed to lie down and take aim. It then rose suddenly, and gave the brig, which was chubby as a cherub, such a mighty slap on the port cheek that she quivered in every timber. And high over the railing, far in upon the deck, dashed the cold salt spray; the captain had scarcely time to duck his head below the companion.

Ah, how refreshing it was! It exhilarated both old and young; they had not had a taste of the cold sea-water for a long time, and with one voice the whole crew broke into a lusty 'Hurrah!'

But at this moment the steerman's stentorian voice rang out: 'Hard to leeward!' The brig luffed up close to the wind, the sails flapped so violently that the rigging shook, and now followed in rapid succession, even quicker than before, orders to anchor. 'Let fall the port anchor! Let go the starboard one too!'

Plump—fell the one; plump—went the other. The old chains rattled out, and a little red cloud of rust rose up on either side of the bowsprit.

The men, accustomed to obey, worked rapidly without thinking why, and the brig soon rode pretty quietly at her two anchors.

But now, after the work was finished, no one could conceal his astonishment at this sudden anchoring, just off the coast, among islets and skerries. And still more extraordinary seemed the behaviour of those in command. For they both stood right forward, with their backs to the weather, leaning over the railing and staring at the port bow. Some had even thought they had heard the captain cry, 'To the pumps, men,' but this point was never cleared up.

'What the devil can they be doing forward?' said the rash young man.

'They think she struck on a reef when we shipped the big sea,' whispered the cabin-boy.

'Hold your jaw, boy!' said the boatswain.

All the same, the cabin-boy's words passed from mouth to mouth; a little chuckle was heard here and there; the men's faces became more and more ludicrously uneasy, and their suppressed laughter was on the point of bursting forth. Then the steersman was seen to nudge the skipper in the side.

'Yes; but then you must whisper to me,' said the latter.

The steersman nodded, and then the skipper turned to the crew and solemnly spoke as follows:

'Yes, this time, fortunately, everything went well; but now I hope that each of you will have learnt how dangerous it is to lend an ear to these juvenile agitators, who can never be quiet and let evolution, as the steersman says, pursue its natural course. I yielded to your wishes this time, it is true, but not because I approved of your insane rashness; it was simply that I might convince you by — by the logic of events. And see — how did things go? Certainly we have, as by a miracle, been spared the worst; but now we lie here, outside our safe haven, our old anchorage, which we have forsaken to be tossed about on the turbulent waters of the unknown and the untried. But, believe me, henceforth you will find both our excellent steersman and your captain at our post, guarding against such crude, immature projects. And if things go badly with us in days to come, you must all remember that it is entirely your own fault; we wash our hands of the matter.'

Thereupon he strode through the men, who respectfully fell back to let him pass. The steersman, who had really whispered, dried his eyes and followed. They both disappeared in the cabin.

There was much strife in the forecastle that day, and it grew worse after.

The brig's happy days were all over. Dissension and discontent, suspicion and obstinacy, converted the narrow limits of the forecastle into a veritable hell.

Only skipper and steersman seemed to thrive well under all this. The general dissatisfaction did not affect them; for they, of course, were not to blame.

None thought of any change. The crew had done what they could, and the skipper, on his part, had also been accommodating.

Now they might keep their minds at rest. The brig lay in a dangerous place, but now she would have to lie — and there she lies to this day.

A DINNER.

There was a large dinner-party at the merchant's. The judge had made a speech in honour of the home-coming of the student, the eldest son of the house, and the merchant had replied with another in honour of the judge; so far all was well and good. And yet one could see that the host was disquieted about something. He answered inconsequentially, decanted Rhine wine into port, and betrayed absence of mind in all manner of ways.

He was meditating upon a speech—a speech beyond the scope of the regulation after-dinner orations. This was something very remarkable; for the merchant was no speaker, and—what was still more remarkable—he knew it himself.

When, therefore, well on in the dinner, he hammered upon the table for silence, and said that he must give expression to a sentiment that lay at his heart, everybody instantly felt that something unusual was impending.

There fell such a sudden stillness upon the table, that one could hear the lively chatter of the ladies, who, in accordance with Norse custom, were dining in the adjoining rooms.

At length the silence reached even them, and they crowded in the doorway to listen. Only the hostess held back, sending her husband an anxious look. 'Ah, dear me!' she sighed, half aloud, 'he is sure to make a muddle of it. He has already made all his speeches; what would he be at now?'

And he certainly did not begin well. He stammered, cleared his throat, got entangled among the usual toast expressions, such as 'I will not fail to—ahem—I am impelled to express my, my—that is, I would beg you, gentlemen, to assist me in—'

The gentlemen sat and stared down into their glasses, ready to empty them upon the least hint of a conclusion. But none came. On the contrary, the speaker recovered himself.

For something really lay at his heart. His joy and pride over his son, who had come home sound and well after having passed a respectable examination, the judge's flattering speech, the good cheer, the wine, the festive mood—all this put words into his mouth. And when he got over the fatal introductory phrases, the words came more and more fluently.

It was the toast of 'The Young.' The speaker dwelt upon our responsibility towards children, and the many sorrows — but also the many joys — that the parents have in them.

He was from time to time compelled to talk quickly to hide his emotion, for he felt what he said.

And when he came to the grown-up children, when he imagined his dear son a partner in his business, and spoke of grandchildren and so on, his words acquired a ring of eloquence which astonished all his hearers, and his peroration was greeted with hearty applause.

'For, gentlemen, it is in these children that we, as it were, continue our existence. We leave them not only our name, but also our work. And we leave them this, not that they may idly enjoy its fruits, but that they may continue it, extend it — yes, do it much better than their fathers were able to. For it is our hope that the rising generation may appropriate the fruits of the work of the age, that they may be freed from the prejudices that have darkened the past and partially darken the present; and, in drinking the health of the young, let us wish that, steadily progressing, they may become worthy of their sires — yes, let us say it — outgrow them.

'And only when we know that we leave the work of our generation in abler hands, can we calmly look forward to the time when we shall bid adieu to our daily task, and then we may confidently reckon upon a bright and glorious future for our dear Fatherland. A health to the Young!'

The hostess, who had ventured nearer when she heard that the speech was going on well, was proud of her husband; the whole company was in an exhilarated humour, but the gladdest of all was the student.

He had stood a little in awe of his father, whose severely patriarchal principles he well knew. He now heard that the old man was extremely liberal-minded towards youth, and he was very glad to be enabled to discourse with him upon serious matters.

But, for the moment, it was only a question of jesting; *à propos* of the toast, there ensued one of those interesting table-talks, about who was really young and who old. After the company had arrived at this witty result, that the eldest were in reality the youngest, they adjourned to the dessert-table, which was laid in the ladies' room.

But, no matter how gallant the gentlemen—especially those of the old school—may be towards the fair sex, neither feminine amiability nor the most *recherché* dessert has power to stop them for long on their way to the smoking-room. And soon the first faint aroma of cigars, so great a luxury to smokers, announced the beginning of that process which has obtained for our ladies the fame of being quite smoke-dried.

The student and a few other young gentlemen remained for a time with the young ladies—under the strict surveillance of the elder ones. But little by little they also were swallowed up in the gray cloud which indicated the way that their fathers had taken.

In the smoking-room they were carrying on a very animated conversation upon some matter of social politics. The host, who was speaking, supported his view with a number of 'historical facts,' which, however, were entirely unreliable.

His opponent, a solicitor of the High Court, was sitting chuckling inwardly at the prospect of refuting these inaccurate statements, when the student entered the room.

He came just in time to hear his father's blundering, and, in his jovial humour, in his delight over the new conception of his father that he had acquired after the toast, he said, with a cheery bluntness:

'Excuse me, father, you are mistaken there. The circumstances are not at all as you state. On the contrary—'

He got no further: the father laughingly slapped him on the shoulder, and said:

'There, there! are you, too, trifling with newspapers! But really, you must not disturb us; we are in the middle of a serious discussion.'

The son heard an irritating sniff from the gray cloud; he was provoked at the scorn implied in his interposition being regarded as disturbing a serious conversation.

He therefore replied somewhat sharply.

The father, who instantly remarked the tone, suddenly changed his own manner.

'Are you serious in coming here and saying that your father is talking nonsense?'

'I did not say that; I only said that you were mistaken.'

'The words are of little moment, but the meaning was there,' said the merchant, who was beginning to get angry. For he heard a gentleman say to his neighbour:

'If this had only happened in my father's time!'

One word now drew forth another, and the situation became extremely painful.

The hostess, who had always an attentive ear for the gentlemen's conversation, as she knew her husband's hasty temper, immediately came and looked in at the door.

'What is it, Adjunct [Footnote: Assistant-teacher.] Hansen?'

'Ah,' replied Hansen, 'your son has forgotten himself a little.'

'To his own father! He must have had too much to drink. Dear Hansen, try and get him out.'

The Adjunct, who was more well-meaning than diplomatic, and who, besides (a rarer thing with old teachers than is generally supposed) was esteemed by his former pupils, went and took the student without ceremony by the arm, saying: 'Come, shall we two take a turn in the garden?'

The young man turned round violently, but when he saw that it was the old teacher, and received, at the same time, a troubled, imploring glance from his mother, he passively allowed himself to be led away.

While in the doorway, he heard the lawyer, whom he had never been able to endure, say something about the egg that would teach the hen to lay, which witticism was received with uproarious laughter. A thrill passed through him; but the Adjunct held him firmly, and out they went.

It was long before the old teacher could get him sufficiently quieted to become susceptible to reason. The disappointment, the bitter sense of being at variance with his father, and, not least, the affront of being treated as a boy in the presence of so many—all this had to pour out for awhile.

But at last he became calm, and sat down with his old friend, who now pointed out to him that it must be very painful to an elderly man to be corrected by a mere youth.

'Yes, but I was right,' said the student, certainly for the twentieth time.

'Good, good! but yet you must not put on an air of wanting to be wiser than your own father.'

'Why, my father himself said that he would have it so.'

'What? When did your father say that?' The teacher almost began to believe that the wine had gone to the young gentleman's head.

'At the table—in his speech.'

'At the table—yes! In his speech—yes! But, don't you see, that is quite another matter. People allow themselves to say such things, especially in speeches; but it is by no means intended that these theories should be translated into practice. No, believe me, my dear boy, I am old, and I know humanity. The world must wag like this; we are not made otherwise. In youth one has his own peculiar view of life, but, young man, it is not the right one. Only when one has arrived at the calm restfulness of an advanced age does one see circumstances in the true light. And now I will tell you something, upon the truth of which you may confidently rely. When you come to your father's years and position, your opinions will be quite the same as his now are, and, like him, you will strive to maintain them and impress them upon your children.'

'No, never! I swear it,' cried the young man, springing to his feet. And now he spoke in glowing terms, to the effect that for him right would always be right, that he would respect the truth, no matter whence it came, that he would respect the young, and so on. In short, he talked as hopeful youths are wont to talk after a good dinner and violent mental disturbance.

He was beautiful, as he stood there with the evening sun shining upon his blonde hair, and his enthusiastic countenance turned upward.

There was in his whole personality and in his words something transporting and convincing, something that could not fail to work an impression—that is to say, if anybody but the teacher had seen and heard him.

For upon the teacher it made no impression whatever; he was old, of course.

The drama of which he had that day been a witness he had seen many times. He himself had successively played both the principal *rôles*; he had seen many *débutants* like the student and many old players like the merchant.

Therefore he shook his venerable head, and said to himself:

'Yes, yes; it is all well enough. But just see if I am not right; he will become precisely the same as the rest of us.'

And the teacher was right.

TROFAST.

[Footnote: Faithful.]

I.

Miss Thyra went and called into the speaking-tube:

'Will Trofast's cutlets be ready soon?'

The maid's voice came up from the kitchen: 'They are on the window-sill cooling; as soon as they are all right, Stine shall bring them up.'

Trofast, who had heard this, went and laid himself quietly down upon the hearthrug.

He understood much better than a human being, the merchant used to say.

Besides the people of the house, there sat at the breakfast-table an old enemy of Trofast's—the only one he had. But be it said that Cand. jur. [Footnote: Graduate in law.] Viggo Hansen was the enemy of a great deal in this world, and his snappish tongue was well known all over Copenhagen. Having been a friend of the family for many years, he affected an especial frankness in this house, and when he was in a querulous mood (which was always the case) he wreaked his bitterness unsparingly upon anything or anybody.

In particular, he was always attacking Trofast.

'That big yellow beast,' he used to say, 'is being petted and pampered and stuffed with steak and cutlets, while many a human child must bite its fingers after a piece of dry bread.'

This, however, was a tender point, of which Dr. Hansen had to be rather careful.

Whenever anyone mentioned Trofast in words that were not full of admiration, he received a simultaneous look from the whole family, and the merchant had even said point-blank to Dr. Hansen that he might one day get seriously angry if the other would not refer to Trofast in a becoming manner.

But Miss Thyra positively hated Dr. Hansen for this; and although Waldemar was now grown up—a student, at any rate—he took a special pleasure in stealing the gloves out of the doctor's back pocket, and delivering them to Trofast to tear.

Yes, the good-wife herself, although as mild and sweet as tea, was sometimes compelled to take the doctor to task, and seriously remonstrate with him for daring to speak so ill of the dear animal.

All this Trofast understood very well; but he despised Dr. Hansen, and took no notice of him. He condescended to tear the gloves, because it pleased his friend Waldemar, but otherwise he did not seem to see the doctor.

When the cutlets came, Trofast ate them quietly and discreetly. He did not crunch the bones, but picked them quite clean, and licked the platter.

Thereupon he went up to the merchant, and laid his right forepaw upon his knee.

'Welcome, welcome, old boy!' cried the merchant with emotion. He was moved in like manner every morning, when this little scene was re-enacted.

'Why, you can't call Trofast old, father,' said Waldemar, with a little tone of superiority.

'Indeed! Do you know that he will soon be eight?'

'Yes, my little man,' said the good wife gently; 'but a dog of eight is not an old dog.'

'No, mother,' exclaimed Waldemar eagerly. 'You side with me, don't you? A dog of eight is not an old dog.'

And in an instant the whole family was divided into two parties—two very ardent parties, who, with an unceasing flow of words, set to debating the momentous question:—whether one can call a dog of eight years an old dog or not. Both sides became warm, and, although each one kept on repeating his unalterable opinion into his opponent's face, it did not seem likely that they would ever arrive at unanimity—not even when old grandmother hurriedly rose from her chair, and positively insisted upon telling some story about the Queen-Dowager's lap-dog, which she had had the honour of knowing from the street.

But in the midst of the irresistible whirl of words there came a pause. Some one looked at his watch and said: 'The steamboat.' They all rose; the gentlemen, who had to go to town, rushed off; the whole company was scattered to the four winds, and the problem — whether one can call a dog of eight an old dog or not — floated away in the air, unsolved.

Trofast alone did not stir. He was accustomed to this domestic din, and these unsolved problems did not interest him. He ran his wise eyes over the deserted breakfast-table, dropped his black nose upon his powerful fore-paws, and closed his eyes for a little morning nap. As long as they were staying out in the country, there was nothing much for him to do, except eat and sleep.

Trofast was one of the pure Danish hounds from the Zoological Gardens. The King had even bought his brother, which fact was expressly communicated to all who came to the house.

All the same, he had had a pretty hard upbringing, for he was originally designated to be watch-dog at the merchant's large coalstore out at Kristianshavn.

Out there, Trofast's behaviour was exemplary. Savage and furious as a tiger at night, in the daytime he was so quiet, kindly, and even humble, that the merchant took notice of him, and promoted him to the position of house-dog.

And it was really from this moment that the noble animal began to develop all his excellent qualities.

From the very beginning he had a peculiar, modest way of standing at the drawing-room door, and looking so humbly at anybody who entered that it was quite impossible to avoid letting him into the room. And there he soon made himself at home — under the sofa at first, but afterwards upon the soft carpet in front of the fire.

And as the other members of the family learned to appreciate his rare gifts, Trofast gradually advanced in importance, until Dr. Hansen maintained that he was the real master of the house.

Certain it is that there came a something into Trofast's whole demeanour which distinctly indicated that he was well aware of the position he occupied. He no longer stood humbly at the door, but entered first himself as soon as it was opened. And if the door was not opened for him instantly when he scratched at it, the powerful animal would raise himself upon his hind-legs, lay his fore-paws upon the latch, and open it for himself.

The first time that he performed this feat the good-wife delightedly exclaimed:

'Isn't he charming? He's just like a human being, only so much better and more faithful!'

The rest of the family were also of opinion that Trofast was better than a human being. Each one seemed, as it were, to get quit of a few of his own sins and infirmities through this admiring worship of the noble animal; and whenever anybody was displeased with himself or others, Trofast received the most confidential communications, and solemn assurances that he was really the only friend upon whom one could rely.

When Miss Thyra came home disappointed from a ball, or when her best friend had faithlessly betrayed a frightfully great secret, she would throw herself, weeping, upon Trofast's neck, and say: 'Now, Trofast, I have only you left. There is nobody—nobody—nobody on the earth who likes me but you! Now we two are quite alone in the wide, wide world; but you will not betray your poor little Thyra— you must promise me that, Trofast.' And so she would weep on, until her tears trickled down Trofast's black nose.

No wonder, therefore, that Trofast comported himself with a certain dignity at home in the house. But in the street also it was evident that he felt self-confident, and that he was proud of being a dog in a town where dogs are in power.

When they were staying in the country in summer, Trofast went to town only once a week or so, to scent out old acquaintances. Out in the country, he lived exclusively for the sake of his health; he bathed, rolled in the flower-beds, and then went into the parlour to rub himself dry upon the furniture, the ladies, and finally upon the hearthrug.

But for the remainder of the year the whole of Copenhagen was at his disposal, and he availed himself of his privileges with much assurance.

What a treat it was, early in the spring, when the fine grass began to shoot upon the public lawns, which no human foot must tread, to run up and down and round in a ring with a few friends, scattering the tufts of grass in the air!

Or when the gardener's people had gone home to dinner, after having pottered and trimmed all the forenoon among the fine flowers and bushes, what fun it was to pretend to dig for moles; thrust his nose down into the earth in the centre of the flower-bed, snort and blow, then begin scraping up the earth with his fore-feet, stop for a little, thrust his muzzle down again, blow, and then fall to digging up earth with all his might, until the hole was so deep that a single vigorous kick from his hind-legs could throw a whole rose-bush, roots and all, high in the air!

When Trofast, after such an escapade, lay quietly in the middle of the lawn, in the warm spring sunshine, and saw the humans trudge wearily past outside, in dust or mud, he would silently and self-complacently wag his tail.

Then there were the great fights in Grönningen, or round the horse in Kongens Nytorv. [Footnote: King's Square.] From thence, wet and bedraggled, he would dash up Östergade [Footnote: East Street.] among people's legs, rubbing against ladies' dresses and gentlemen's trousers, overthrowing old women and children, exercising an unlimited right-of-way on both sides of the pavement, now rushing into a backyard and up the kitchen stairs after a cat, now scattering terror and confusion by flying right at the throat of an old enemy. Or Trofast would sometimes amuse himself by stopping in front of a little girl who might be going an errand for her mother, thrusting his black nose up into her face, and growling, with gaping jaws, 'Bow, wow, wow!'

If you could see the little thing! She becomes blue in the face, her arms hang rigidly by her sides, her feet keep tripping up and down; she tries to scream, but cannot utter a sound.

But the grown ladies in the street cry shame upon her, and say:

'What a little fool! How *can* you be afraid of such a dear, nice dog? Why, he only wants to play with you! See what a great big, fine fellow he is. Won't you pat him?'

But this the little one will not do upon any account; and, when she goes home to her mother, the sobs are still rising in her throat. Neither her mother nor the doctor can understand, afterwards, why the healthy, lively child becomes rigid and blue in the face at the least fright, and loses the power to scream.

But all these diversions were colourless and tame in comparison with *les grands cavalcades d'amour*, in which Trofast was always one of the foremost. Six, eight, ten, or twelve large yellow, black, and red dogs, with a long following of smaller and quite small ones, so bitten and mud-bespattered that one could scarcely see what they were made of, but yet very courageous, tails in the air and panting with ardour, although they stood no chance at all, except of getting mauled again and rolled in the mud. And so off in a wild gallop through streets, squares, gardens, and flower-beds, fighting and howling, covered with blood and dirt, tongues lolling from mouths. Out of the way with humans and baby-carriages, room for canine warfare and love! And thus they would rush on like Aasgaard's demon riders [Footnote: Aasgaard was the 'garth' or home of the gods. After the advent of Christianity, the Norse gods became demons, and it was the popular belief that they rode across the sky at night, foreboding evil.] through the unhappy town.

Trofast heeded none of the people on the street except the policemen. For, with his keen understanding, he had long ago discerned that the police were there to protect him and his kind against the manifold encroachments of humanity. Therefore he obligingly stopped whenever he met a policeman, and allowed himself to be scratched behind the ear. In particular, he had a good, stout friend, whom he often met up in Aabenraa, where he (Trofast) had a *liaison* of many years' standing.

When Policeman Frode Hansen was seen coming upstairs from a cellar—a thing that often happened, for he was a jolly fellow, and it was a pleasure to offer him a half of lager-beer—his face bore a great likeness to the rising sun. It was round and red, warm and beaming.

But when he appeared in full view upon the pavement, casting a severe glance up and down the street, in order to ascertain whether any evil-disposed person had seen where he came from, there would arise a faint reminiscence of something that we, as young men, had read about in physics, and which, I believe, we called the co-efficient of expansion.

For, when we looked at the deep incision made by his strong belt, before, behind and at the sides, we involuntarily received the impression that such a co-efficient, with an extraordinarily strong tendency to expand, was present in Frode Hansen's stomach.

And people who met him, especially when he heaved one of his deep, beery sighs, nervously stepped to one side. For if the co-efficient in there should ever happen to get the better of the strong belt, the pieces, and particularly the front buckle, would fly around with a force sufficient to break plate-glass windows.

In other respects, Frode Hansen was not very dangerous of approach. He was even looked upon as one of the most harmless of police-constables; he very rarely reported a case of any kind. All the same, he stood well with his superiors, for when anything was reported by others, no matter what, if they only asked Frode Hansen, he could always make some interesting disclosure or other about it.

In this way the world went well with him; he was almost esteemed in Aabenraa and down Vognmagergade. Yes, even Mam Hansen sometimes found means to stand him a half of lager beer.

And she had certainly little to give away. Poverty-stricken and besotted, she had enough to do to struggle along with her two children.

Not that Mam Hansen worked or tried to work herself forward or upward; if she could only manage to pay her rent and have a little left over for coffee and brandy, she was content. Beyond this she had no illusions.

In reality, the general opinion — even in Aabenraa — was that Mam Hansen was a beast; and, when she was asked if she were a widow, she would answer: 'Well, you see, that's not so easy to know.'

The daughter was about fifteen and the son a couple of years younger. About these, too, the public opinion of Aabenraa and district had it that a worse pair of youngsters had seldom grown up in those parts.

Waldemar was a little, pale, dark-eyed fellow, slippery as an eel, full of mischief and cunning, with a face of indiarubber, which in one second could change its expression from the boldest effrontery to the most sheepish innocence.

Nor was there anything good to say about Thyra, except that she gave promise of becoming a pretty girl. But all sorts of ugly stories were already told about her, and she gadded round the town upon very various errands.

Mam Hansen would never listen to these stories; she merely waved them off. She paid just as little attention to the advice of her female friends and neighbours, when they said:

'Let the children shift for themselves—really, they're quite brazen enough to do it—and take in a couple of paying lodgers.'

'No, no,' Mam Hansen would reply; 'as long as they have some kind of a home with me, the police will not get a firm grip of them, and they will not quite flow over.'

This idea, that the bairns should not quite 'flow over,' had grown and grown in her puny brain, until it had become the last point, around which gathered everything motherly that could be left, after a life like hers.

And therefore she slaved on, scolded and slapped the children when they came late home, made their bed, gave them a little food, and so held them to her, in some kind of fashion.

Mam Hansen had tried many things in the course of her life, and everything had brought her gradually downward, from servant-girl to waitress, down past washerwoman to what she now was.

Early in the mornings, before it was light, she would come over Knippelsbro [Footnote: Bro, a bridge.] into the town, with a heavy basket upon each arm. Out of the baskets stuck cabbage-leaves and carrot-tops, so that one would suppose that she made a business of buying vegetables from the peasants out at Amager, in order to sell them in Aabenraa and the surrounding quarters.

All the same, it was not a greengrocery business that she carried on, but, on the contrary, a little coal business: she sold coals clandestinely and in small portions to poor folk like herself.

This evident incongruity was not noticed in Aabenraa; not even Policeman Frode Hansen seemed to find anything remarkable about Mam Hansen's business. When he met her in the mornings, toiling along with the heavy baskets, he usually asked quite genially: 'Well, my little Mam Hansen, were the roots cheap to-day?'

And, if his greeting were less friendly than usual, he was treated to a half of lager later in the day.

This was a standing outlay of Madam Hansen's, and she had one besides. Every evening she bought a large piece of sugared Vienna bread. She did not eat it herself; neither was it for the children; no one knew what she did with it, nor did anybody particularly care.

When there was no prospect of halves of lager, Policeman Frode Hansen promenaded his co-efficient with dignity up and down the street.

If he then happened to meet Trofast or any other of his canine friends, he always made a long halt, for the purpose of scratching him behind the ear. And when he observed the great *nonchalance* with which the dogs comported themselves in the street, it was a real pleasure to him to sternly pounce upon some unhappy man and note down his full name and address, because he had taken the liberty of throwing an envelope into the gutter.

II.

It was late in the autumn. There was a dinner-party at the merchant's; the family had been back from the country for some time.

The conversation flowed on languidly and intermittently, until the flood-gates were suddenly lifted, and it became a wild *fos* [Footnote: Waterfall, cataract.] For down at the hostess's end of the table this question had cropped up: 'Can one call a lady a fine lady — a real fine lady — if it be known that on a steam-boat she has put her feet up on a stool, and disclosed small shoes and embroidered stockings?' And, strangely enough, as if each individual in the company had spent half his life in considering and weighing this question, all cast their matured, decided, unalterable opinions upon the table. The opposing parties were formed in an instant; the unalterable opinions collided with each other, fell down, were caught up again, and thrown with ever-increasing ardour.

Up at the other end of the table they took no part in this animated conversation. Near the host there sat mostly elderly gentlemen, and however ardently their wives might have desired to solve the problem once for all by expressing their unalterable opinion, they were compelled to give up the idea, as the focus of the animated conversation was among some young students right down beside the hostess, and the distance was too great.

'I don't think I see the big yellow beast to-day,' said Dr. Viggo Hansen in his querulous tone.

'Unfortunately not. Trofast is not here to-day. Poor fellow! I have been obliged to request him to do me a disagreeable service.'

The merchant always talked about Trofast as if he were an esteemed business friend.

'You make me quite curious. Where *is* the dear animal?'

'Ah, my dear madam, it is indeed a tiresome story. For, you know, there has been stealing going on out at our coal warehouse at Kristianshavn.'

'Oh, good gracious! Stealing?'

'The thefts have evidently been practised systematically for a long time.'

'Have you noticed the stock getting less, then?'

But now the merchant had to laugh, which he seldom did.

'No, no, my dear doctor, excuse my laughing, but you are really too naive. Why, there are now about ten thousand tons of coal out there, so you will see that it wants some—'

'They would have to steal from evening till morning with a pair of horses,' interjected a young business man, who was witty.

When the merchant had finished his laugh, he continued:

'No; the theft was discovered by means of a little snow that fell yesterday.'

'What! Snow yesterday? I don't know anything about that.'

'It was not at the time of day when we are awake, madam, it is true; but yet, very early yesterday morning there fell a little snow, and when my folks arrived at the coal store, they discovered the footprints of the thief or thieves. It was then found that a couple of boards in the wall were loose, but they had been so skilfully put in place that nobody would ever notice anything wrong. And the thief crawls through the opening night after night; is it not outrageous?'

'But don't you keep a watch-dog?'

'Certainly I do; but he is a young animal (of excellent breed, by the way, half a bloodhound), and, whatever way these wretches go about their work, it is evident that they must be on friendly terms with the beast, for the dog's footprints were found among those of the thieves.'

'That was indeed remarkable. And now Trofast is to try what he can do, I presume?'

'Yes, you are quite right. I have sent Trofast out there to-day; he will catch the villains for me.'

'Could you not nail the loose boards securely in position?'

'Of course we could, Dr. Hansen; but I must get hold of the fellows. They shall have their well-merited punishment. My sense of right is most deeply wounded.'

'It is really delightful to have such a faithful animal.'

'Yes, isn't it, madam? We men must confess to our shame that in many respects we are far behind the dumb animals.'

'Yes, Trofast is really a pearl, sir. He is, beyond comparison, the prettiest dog in all—'

'Constantinople,' interrupted Dr. Hansen.

'That is an old joke of Hansen's,' explained the merchant. 'He has re-christened the Northern Athens the Northern Constantinople, because he thinks there are too many dogs.'

'It is good for the dog-tax,' said some one.

'Yes, if the dog-tax were not so inequitably fixed,' snapped Dr. Hansen. 'There is really no sense in a respectable old lady, who keeps a dog in a hand-bag, having to pay as much as a man who takes pleasure in annoying his fellow-creatures by owning a half-wild animal as big as a little lion.'

'May I ask how you would have the dog-tax reckoned, Dr. Hansen?'

'According to weight, of course,' replied Dr. Viggo Hansen without hesitation.

The old merchants and councillors laughed so heartily at this idea of weighing the dogs, that the disputants at the lower end of the table, who were still vigorously bombarding each other with unalterable opinions, became attentive and dropped their opinions, in order to listen to the discussion on dogs. And the question, 'Can one call a lady a fine lady—a really fine lady—if it be known that on a steamboat she has put her feet up on a stool, and disclosed small shoes and embroidered stockings?' also floated away in the air, unsolved.

'You seem to be a downright hater of dogs, Dr. Hansen!' said the lady next to him, still laughing.

'I must tell you, madam,' cried a gentleman across the table, 'that he is terribly afraid of dogs.'

'But one thing,' continued the lady—'one thing you must admit, and that is, that the dog has always been the faithful companion of man.'

'Yes, that is true, madam, and I could tell you what the dog has learned from man, and man from the dog.'

'Tell us; do tell us!' was simultaneously exclaimed from several quarters.

'With pleasure. In the first place, man has taught the dog to fawn.'

'What a very queer thing to say!' cried old grandmother.

'Next, the dog has acquired all the qualities that make man base and unreliable: cringing flattery upward, and rudeness and contempt downward; the narrowest adhesion to his own, and distrust and hatred of all else. Indeed, the noble animal has proved such an apt pupil that he even understands the purely human art of judging people by their clothes. He lets well-dressed folks alone, but snaps at the legs of the ragged.'

Here the doctor was interrupted by a general chorus of disapproval, and Miss Thyra bitterly gripped the fruit-knife in her little hand.

But there were some who wanted to hear what mankind had learned from the dog, and Dr. Hansen proceeded, with steadily-growing passion and bitterness:

'Man has learned from the dog to set a high price upon this grovelling, unmerited worship. When neither injustice nor ill-treatment has ever met anything but this perpetually wagging tail, stomach upon earth, and licking tongue, the final result is that the master fancies himself a splendid fellow, to whom all this devotion belongs as a right. And, transferring his experience of the dog into his human intercourse, he puts little restraint upon himself, expecting to meet wagging tails and licking tongues. And if he be disappointed, then he despises mankind and turns, with loud-mouthed eulogies, to the dog.'

He was once more interrupted; some laughed, but the greater number were offended. By this time Viggo Hansen had warmed to his subject; his little, sharp voice pierced through the chorus of objections, and he proceeded as follows:

'And, while we are speaking of the dog, may I be allowed to present an extraordinarily profound hypothesis of my own? Is there not something highly characteristic of our national character in the fact that it is we who have produced this noble breed of dogs—the celebrated, pure Danish hounds? This strong, broad-chested animal with the heavy paws, the black throat, and the frightful teeth, but so good-natured, harmless, and amiable withal—does he not remind you of the renowned, indestructible Danish loyalty, which has never met injustice or ill-treatment with anything but perpetually wagging tail, stomach upon earth, and licking tongue? And when we admire this animal, formed in our own image, is it not with a kind of melancholy self-praise that we pat him upon the head, and say: "You are indeed a great, good, faithful creature!"'

'Do you hear, Dr. Hansen? I must point out to you that in my house there are certain matters which—'

The host was angry, but a good-natured relation of the family hastened to interrupt him, saying: 'I am a countryman, and you will surely admit, Dr. Hansen, that a good farm watch-dog is an absolute necessity for *us*. Eh?'

'Oh yes, a little cur that can yelp, so as to awake the master.'

'No, thank you. We must have a decent dog, that can lay the rascals by the heels. I have now a magnificent bloodhound.'

'And if an honest fellow comes running up to tell you that your outbuildings are burning, and your magnificent bloodhound flies at his throat—what then?'

'Why, that would be awkward,' laughed the countryman. And the others laughed too.

Dr. Hansen was now so busily engaged in replying to all sides, employing the most extravagant paradoxes, that the young folks in particular were extremely amused, without specially noting the increasing bitterness of his tone.

'But our watch-dogs, our watch-dogs! You will surely let us keep them, doctor?' exclaimed a coal-merchant laughingly.

'Not at all. Nothing is more unreasonable than that a poor man, who comes to fill his bag from a coal mountain, should be torn to pieces by wild beasts. There is absolutely no reasonable relation between such a trifling misdemeanour and so dreadful a punishment.'

'May we ask how you would protect your coal mountain, if you had one?'

'I should erect a substantial fence of boards, and if I were very anxious, I should keep a watchman, who would say politely, but firmly, to those who came with bags: "Excuse me, but my master is very particular about that. You must not fill your bag; you must take yourself off at once."'

Through the general laughter which followed this last paradox, a clerical gentleman spoke from the ladies' end of the table:

'It appears to me that there is something lacking in this discussion—something that I would call the ethical aspect of the question. Is it not a fact that in the hearts of all who sit here there is a clear, definite sense of the revolting nature of the crime we call theft?'

These words were received with general and hearty applause.

'And I think it does very great violence to our feelings to hear Dr. Hansen minimising a crime that is distinctly mentioned in Divine and human law as one of the worst—to hear him reduce it to the size of a trifling and insignificant misdemeanour. Is not this highly demoralizing and dangerous to Society?'

'Permit me, too,' promptly replied the indefatigable Hansen, 'to present an ethical aspect of the question. Is it not a fact that in the hearts of innumerable persons who do not sit here there is a clear, definite sense of the revolting nature of the crime they call wealth? And must it not greatly outrage the feelings of those who do not themselves possess any coal except an empty bag, to see a man who permits himself to own two or three hundred thousand sacks letting wild beasts loose to guard his coal mountain, and then going to bed after having written on the gate: "Watch-dogs unfastened at dusk"? Is not that very provoking and very dangerous to Society?'

'Oh, good God and Father! He is a regular *sans-culotte*!' cried old grandmother.

The majority gave vent to mutterings of displeasure; he was going too far; it was no longer amusing. Only a few still laughingly exclaimed: 'He does not mean a word of what he says; it is only his way. Good health, Hansen!'

But the host took the matter more seriously. He thought of himself, and he thought of Trofast. With ominous politeness, he began:

'May I venture to ask what you understand by a reasonable relation between a crime and its punishment?'

'For example,' replied Dr. Viggo Hansen, who was now thoroughly roused, 'if I heard that a merchant possessing two or three hundred thousand sacks of coal had refused to allow a poor creature to fill his bag, and that this same merchant, as a punishment, had been torn to pieces by wild beasts, then that would be something that I could very easily understand, for between such heartlessness and so horrible a punishment there is a reasonable relation.'

'Ladies and gentlemen, my wife and I beg you to make yourselves at home, and welcome.'

There was a secret whispering and muttering, and a depressed feeling among the guests, as they dispersed themselves through the salons.

The host walked about with a forced smile on his lips, and, as soon as he had welcomed every one individually, he went in search of Hansen, in order to definitely show him the door once for all.

But this was not necessary. Dr. Viggo Hansen had already found it.

III.

There had really been some snow, as the merchant had stated. Although it was so early in the winter, a little wet snow fell towards morning for several days in succession, but it turned into fine rain when the sun rose.

This was almost the only sign that the sun had risen, for it did not get much lighter or warmer all day. The air was thick with fog — not the whitish-gray sea mist, but brown-gray, close, dead Russian fog, which had not become lighter in passing over Sweden; and the east wind came with it and packed it well and securely down among the houses of Copenhagen.

Under the trees along Kastelgraven and in Gronningen the ground was quite black after the dripping from the branches. But along the middle of the streets and on the roofs there was a thin white layer of snow.

All was yet quite still over at Burmeister and Wain's; the black morning smoke curled up from the chimneys, and the east wind dashed it down upon the white roofs. Then it became still blacker, and spread over the harbour among the rigging of the ships, which lay sad and dark in the gray morning light, with white streaks of snow along their sides. At the Custom House the bloodhounds would soon be shut in, and the iron gates opened.

The east wind was strong, rolling the waves in upon Langelinie, and breaking them in grayish-green foam among the slimy stones, whilst long swelling billows dashed into the harbour, broke under the Custom House, and rolled great names and gloomy memories over the stocks round the fleet's anchorage, where lay the old dismantled wooden frigates in all their imposing uselessness.

The harbour was still full of ships, and goods were piled high in the warehouses and upon the quays.

Nobody could know what kind of winter they were to have — whether they would be cut off for months from the world, or if it would go by with fogs and snow-slush.

Therefore there lay row upon row of petroleum casks, which, together with the enormous coal mountains, awaited a severe winter, and there lay pipes and hogsheads of wine and cognac, patiently waiting for new adulterations; oil and tallow and cork and iron—all lay and waited, each its own destiny.

Everywhere lay work waiting—heavy work, coarse work, and fine work, from the holds of the massive English coal-steamers, right up to the three gilded cupolas on the Emperor of Russia's new church in Bredgade.

But as yet there was no one to put a hand to all this work. The town slept heavily, the air was thick, winter hung over the city, and it was so still in the streets that one could hear the water from the melting snow on the roofs fall down into the spouts with a deep gurgling, as if even the great stone houses yet sobbed in semi-slumber.

A little sleepy morning clock chimed over upon Holmen; here and there a door was opened, and a dog came out to howl; curtains were rolled up and windows were opened; the servant-girls went about in the houses, and did their cleaning by a naked light which stood and flickered; at a window in the palace sat a gilded lacquey and rubbed his nose in that early morning hour.

The fog lay thick over the harbour, and hung in the rigging of the great ships as if in a forest; rain and flakes of wet snow made it still thicker, but the east wind pressed it down between the houses, and completely filled Amalieplads, so that Frederick V. sat as if in the clouds, and turned his proud nose unconcernedly towards his half-finished church.

Some more sleepy clocks now began to chime; a steam-whistle joined in with a diabolical shriek. In the taverns which 'open before the clock strikes' they were already serving early refections of hot coffee and schnapps; girls with hair hanging down their backs, after a wild night, came out of the sailors' houses by Nyhavn, and sleepily began to clean windows.

It was bitterly cold and raw, and those who had to cross Kongens Nytorv hurried past Öhlenschläger, whom they had set outside the theatre, bare-headed, with his collar full of snow, which melted and ran down into his open shirt-front.

Now came the long, relentless blasts of steam-whistles from the factories all round the town, and the little steamers in the harbour whistled for no reason at all.

The work, which everywhere lay waiting, began to swallow up the many small dark figures, who, sleepy and freezingly cold, appeared and disappeared all round the town. And there was almost a quiet bustle in the streets; some ran, others walked — both those who had to go down into the coal steamers, and those who must up and gild the Emperor of Russia's cupolas, and thousands of others who were being swallowed by all kinds of work.

And waggons began to rumble, criers to shout, engines raised their polished, oily shoulders, and turned their buzzing wheels; and little by little the heavy, thick atmosphere was filled with a muffled murmur from the collective work of thousands. The day was begun; joyous Copenhagen was awake.

Policeman Frode Hansen froze even to his innermost co-efficient. It had been an unusually bitter watch, and he walked impatiently up and down in Aabenraa, and waited for Mam Hansen. She was in the habit of coming at this time, or even earlier, and to-day he had almost resolved to carry matters as far as a half lager or a cup of warm coffee.

But Mam Hansen came not, and he began to wonder whether it was not really his duty to report her. She was carrying the thing too far; it would not do at all any longer, this humbug with these cabbage-leaves and that coal business.

Thyra and Waldemar had also several times peeped out into the little kitchen, to see if their mother had come and had put the coffee-pot on the fire. But it was black under the kettle, and the air was so dark and the room so cold that they jumped into bed again.

When they opened the great gates of merchant Hansen's coalstore at Kristianshavn, Trofast sat there and shamefacedly looked askance; it was really a loathsome piece of work that they had set him to do.

In a corner, between two empty baskets, they found a bundle of rags, from which there came a faint moaning. There were a few drops of blood upon the snow, and close by there lay, untouched, a piece of sugared Vienna bread.

When the foreman understood the situation, he turned to Trofast to praise him. But Trofast had already gone home; the position was quite too uncomfortable for *him.*

They gathered her up, such as she was, wet and loathsome, and the foreman decided that she should be placed upon the first coal-cart going into town, and that they could stop at the hospital, so that the professor himself might see whether she was worth repairing.

About ten o'clock the merchant's family began to assemble at the breakfast-table. Thyra came first. She hurried up to Trofast, patted and kissed him, and overwhelmed him with words of endearment.

But Trofast did not move his tail, and scarcely raised his eyes. He kept on licking his fore-paws, which were a little black after the coal.

'Good gracious, my dear mother!' cried Miss Thyra; 'Trofast is undoubtedly ill. Of course he has caught cold in the night; it was really horrid of father.'

But when Waldemar came in, he declared, with a knowing air, that Trofast was affronted.

All three now fell upon him with entreaties and excuses and kind words, but Trofast coldly looked from one to the other. It was clear that Waldemar was right.

Thyra then ran out for her father, and the merchant came in serious — somewhat solemn. They had just told him by telephone from the office how well Trofast had acquitted himself of his task, and, kneeling down on the hearthrug before Trofast, he thanked him warmly for the great service.

This mollified Trofast a good deal.

Still kneeling, with Trofast's paw in his hand, the merchant now told his family what had occurred during the night. That the thief was a hardened old woman, one of the very worst kind, who had even — just imagine it! — driven a pretty considerable trade in the stolen coal. She had been cunning enough to bribe the young watch-dog with a dainty piece of bread; but, of course, that was no use with Trofast.

'And that brings me to think how often a certain person, whom I do not wish to name, would rant about it being a shame that a beast should refuse bread, for which many a human being would be thankful. Do we not now see the good of that? Through that—ahem!—that peculiarity, Trofast was enabled to reveal an abominable crime; to contribute to the just punishment of evildoers, and thus benefit both us and society.'

'But, father,' exclaimed Miss Thyra, 'will you not promise me one thing?'

'What is that, my child?'

'That you will never again require such a service of Trofast. Rather let them steal a little.'

'That I promise you, Thyra; and you, too, my brave Trofast,' said the merchant, rising with dignity.

'Trofast is hungry,' said Waldemar, with his knowing air.

'Goodness, Thyra! fetch his cutlets!'

Thyra was about to rush down into the kitchen, but at that moment Stine came puffing upstairs with them.

Presumably, the professor did not find Mam Hansen worth repairing. At any rate, she was never seen again, and the children 'flowed quite over.' I do not know what became of them.

KAREN.

[Footnote: The scene of this tale is laid in Denmark.]

There was once in Krarup Kro [Footnote: Kro, a country inn.] a girl named Karen. She had to wait upon all the guests, for the inn-keeper's wife almost always went about looking for her keys. And there came many to Krarup Kro—folk from the surrounding district, who gathered in the autumn gloamings, and sat in the inn parlour drinking coffee-punches, usually without any definite object; and also travellers and wayfarers, who tramped in, blue and weather-beaten, to get something hot to carry them on to the next inn.

But Karen could manage everything all the same, although she walked about so quietly, and never seemed in a hurry.

She was small and slim, quite young, grave and silent, so that with her there was no amusement for the commercial travellers. But decent folks who went into the tavern in earnest, and who set store on their coffee being served promptly and scalding hot, thought a great deal of Karen. And when she slipped quietly forward among the guests with her tray, the unwieldy frieze-clad figures fell back with unaccustomed celerity to make way for her, and the conversation stopped for a moment. All had to look after her, she was so charming.

Karen's eyes were of that large gray sort which seem at once to look at one and to look far, far beyond, and her eyebrows were loftily arched, as if in wonder.

Therefore strangers thought she did not rightly understand what they asked for. But she understood very well, and made no mistakes. There was only something strange about her, as if she were looking for something far away, or listening, or waiting, or dreaming.

The wind came from the west over the low plains. It had rolled long, heavy billows across the Western Sea; [Footnote: German Ocean.] salt and wet with spray and foam, it had dashed in upon the coast. But on the high downs with the tall wrack-grass it had become dry and full of sand and somewhat tired, so that when it came to Krarup Kro it had quite enough to do to open the stable-doors.

But open they flew, and the wind filled the spacious building, and forced its way in at the kitchen-door, which stood ajar. And at last there was such a pressure of air that the doors in the other end of the stable also burst open; and now the west wind rushed triumphantly right through the building, swinging the lantern that hung from the roof, whisking the ostler's cap out into the darkness, blowing the rugs over the horses' heads, and sweeping a white hen off the roost into the watering-trough. And the cock raised a frightful screech, and the ostler swore, and the hens cackled, and in the kitchen they were nearly smothered with smoke, and the horses grew restless, and struck sparks from the stones. Even the ducks, which had huddled themselves together near the mangers, so as to be first at the spilt corn, began quacking; and the wind howled through the stable with a hellish din, until a couple of men came out from the inn parlour, set their broad backs against the doors and pressed them to again, while the sparks from their great tobacco-pipes flew about their beards.

After these achievements the wind plunged down into the heather, ran along the deep ditches, and took a substantial grip of the mail-coach, which it met half a mile from the town.

'He is always in a devil of a hurry to get to Krarup Kro!' growled Anders, the postboy, cracking his whip over the perspiring horses.

For this was certainly the twentieth time that the guard had lowered the window to shout something or other up to Anders. First it was a friendly invitation to a coffee-punch in the inn; but each time the friendliness became scantier, until at last the window was let down with a bang, and out sped some brief but expressive remarks about both driver and horses, which Anders, at all events, could not have cared to hear.

Meanwhile the wind swept low along the ground, and sighed long and strangely in the dry clusters of heather. The moon was full, but so densely beclouded that only a pale hazy shimmer hovered over the night.

Behind Krarup Kro lay a peat moss, dark with black turf-stacks and dangerous deep pits. And among the heathery mounds there wound a strip of grass that looked like a path; but it was no path, for it stopped on the very brink of a turf-pit that was larger than the others, and deeper also.

In this grassy strip the fox lay and lurked, quite flat, and the hare bounded lightly over the heather.

It was easy for the fox to calculate that the hare would not describe a wide circle so late in the evening. It cautiously raised its pointed nose and made an estimate; and as it sneaked back before the wind, to find a good place from which it could see where the hare would finish its circuit and lie down, it self-complacently thought that the foxes were always getting wiser and wiser, and the hares more foolish than ever.

In the inn they were unusually busy, for a couple of commercial travellers had ordered roast hare; besides, the landlord was at an auction in Thisted, and Madame had never been in the habit of seeing to anything but the kitchen. But now it unfortunately chanced that the lawyer wanted to get hold of the landlord, and, as he was not at home, Madame had to receive a lengthy message and an extremely important letter, which utterly bewildered her.

By the stove stood a strange man in oilskins, waiting for a bottle of soda-water; two fish-buyers had three times demanded cognac for their coffee; the stableman stood with an empty lantern waiting for a light, and a tall, hard-featured countryman followed Karen anxiously with his eyes; he had to get sixty-three öre change out of a krone. [Footnote: A krone contains 100 öre, and is equal to 1 S. 1-1/2 d.]

But Karen went to and fro without hurrying herself, and without getting confused. One could scarcely understand how she kept account of all this. The large eyes and the wondering eyebrows were strained as if in expectation. She held her fine little head erect and steady, as if not to be distracted from all she had to think of. Her simple dress of blue serge had become too tight for her, so that the collar cut slightly into her neck, forming a little fold in the skin below the hair.

'These country girls are very white-skinned,' said one of the fish-buyers to the other. They were young men, and talked about Karen as connoisseurs.

At the window was a man who looked at the clock and said: 'The post comes early to-night.'

There was a rumbling of wheels on the paving-stones without, the stable-door was flung open, and the wind again rattled all the doors and drove smoke out of the stove.

Karen slipped out into the kitchen the moment the door of the parlour was opened. The mail-guard entered, and said 'good-evening' to the company.

He was a tall, handsome man, with dark eyes, black curly hair and beard, and a small, well-shaped head. The long rich cloak of King of Denmark's magnificent red cloth was adorned with a broad collar of curled dogskin that drooped over his shoulders.

All the dim, sickly light from the two paraffin lamps that hung over the table seemed to fall affectionately upon the red colour, which contrasted so strikingly with the sober black and gray tints of all else in the room. And the tall figure with the small curly head, the broad collar, and the long purple folds, became, as he walked through the low-roofed, smoky room, a marvel of beauty and magnificence.

Karen came hurriedly in from the kitchen with her tray. She bent her head, so that one could not see her face, as she hastened from guest to guest.

She placed the roast hare right in front of the two fish-buyers, whereupon she took a bottle of soda-water to the two commercial travellers, who sat in the inner room. Then she gave the anxious countryman a tallow candle, and, as she slipped out again, she put sixty-three öre into the hand of the stranger by the stove.

The innkeeper's wife was in utter despair. She had, indeed, quite unexpectedly found her keys, but lost the lawyer's letter immediately after, and now the whole inn was in the most frightful commotion. None had got what they wanted—all were shouting together. The commercial men kept continuously ringing the table bell; the fish-buyers went into fits of laughter over the roast hare, which lay straddling on the dish before them. But the anxious countryman tapped Madame on the shoulder with his tallow candle; he trembled for his sixty-three öre. And, amid all this hopeless confusion, Karen had disappeared without leaving a trace.

Anders the post-boy sat on the box; the innkeeper's boy stood ready to open the gates; the two passengers inside the coach became impatient, as did also the horses—although they had nothing to look forward to—and the wind rustled and whistled through the stable.

At length came the guard, whom they awaited. He carried his large cloak over his arm, as he walked up to the coach and made a little excuse for having kept the party waiting. The light of the lantern shone upon his face; he looked very warm, and smilingly said as much, as he drew on his cloak and climbed up beside the driver.

The gates were opened, and the coach rumbled away. Anders let the horses go gently, for now there was no hurry. Now and then he stole a glance at the guard by his side; he was still sitting smiling to himself, and letting the wind ruffle his hair.

Anders the post-boy also smiled in his peculiar way. He began to understand.

The wind followed the coach until the road turned; thereupon it again swept over the plain, and whistled and sighed long and strangely among the dry clusters of heather. The fox lay at his post; everything was calculated to a nicety; the hare must soon be there.

In the inn Karen had at last reappeared, and the confusion had gradually subsided. The anxious countryman had got quit of his candle and received his sixty-three öre, and the commercial gentlemen had set to work upon the roast hare.

Madame whined a little, but she never scolded Karen; there was not a person in the world who could scold Karen.

Quietly and without haste Karen again walked to and fro, and the air of peaceful comfort that always followed her once more overspread the snug, half-dark parlour. But the two fish-buyers, who had had both one and two cognacs with their coffee, were quite taken up with her. She had got some colour in her cheeks, and wore a little half-hidden gleam of a smile, and when she once happened to raise her eyes, a thrill shot through their whole frames.

But when she felt their eyes following her, she went into the room where the commercial men sat dining, and began to polish some teaspoons at the sideboard.

'Did you notice the mail-guard?' asked one of the travellers.

'No, not particularly; I only got a glimpse of him. I think he went out again directly,' replied the other, with his mouth full of food.

'He's a devilish fine fellow! Why, I danced at his wedding.'

'Indeed. So he is married?'

'Yes; his wife lives in Lemvig; they have at least two children. She was a daughter of the innkeeper of Ulstrop, and I arrived there on the very evening of the wedding. It was a jolly night, you may be sure.'

Karen dropped the teaspoons and went out. She did not hear them calling to her from the parlour. She walked across the court-yard to her chamber, closed the door, and began half-unconsciously to arrange the bedclothes. Her eyes stood rigid in the darkness; she pressed her hands to her head, to her breast; she moaned; she did not understand — she did not understand —

But when she heard Madame calling so piteously, 'Karen, Karen!' she sprang up, rushed out of the yard, round the back of the house, out — out upon the heath.

In the twilight the little grassy strip wound in and out among the heather, as if it were a path; but it was no path — no one must believe it to be a path — for it led to the very brink of the great turf-pit.

The hare started up; it had heard a splash. It dashed off with long leaps, as if mad; now contracted, with legs under body and back arched, now drawn out to an incredible length, like a flying accordion, it bounded away over the heather.

The fox put up its pointed nose, and stared in amazement after the hare. It had not heard any splash. For, according to all the rules of art, it had come creeping along the bottom of a deep ditch; and, as it was not conscious of having made any mistake, it could not understand the strange conduct of the hare.

Long it stood, with its head up, its hindquarters lowered, and its great bushy tail hidden in the heather; and it began to wonder whether the hares were getting wiser or the foxes getting more foolish.

But when the west wind had travelled a long way it became a north wind, then an east wind, then a south wind, and at last it again came over the sea as a west wind, dashed in upon the downs, and sighed long and strangely among the dry clusters of heather. But then a pair of wondering gray eyes were lacking in Krarup Kro, and a blue serge dress that had grown too tight. And the innkeeper's wife whined and whimpered more than ever. She could not understand it—nobody could understand it—except Anders the post-boy—and one beside.

But when old folks wished to give the young a really serious admonition, they used to begin thus: 'There was once in Krarup Kro a girl named Karen——

MY SISTER'S JOURNEY TO MODUM.

My sister was going to Modum. It was before the opening of the Drammen Railway, and it was a dreadfully long carriole drive from Christiania to Drammen.

But everything depended upon getting off—hyp—getting to Drammen—hyp, hyp—in time to catch the train which left for Modum at two o'clock. Hyp—oh, dear, if the train should be gone— to wait until next day—alone—in Drammen!

My sister stimulated the post-boys with drink-money, and the horses with small pokes of her umbrella; but both horses and post-boys were numerous upon this route, and much time was lost at the stopping-places.

First, the luggage had to be transferred to the new carriole. There were the big trunk and the little one, and the plaids with loosened strap, the umbrella, the *en-tout-cas*, the bouquet, and the book.

Then there was paying, and reckoning, and changing; and the purse was crammed so extraordinarily full that it would shower three-skilling pieces, [Footnote: Skilling, a halfpenny.] or a shining half-dollar would swing itself over the side, make a graceful curve, like a skater, round the floor, and disappear behind the stove. It had to be got out before it could be changed, and that nobody could do.

As soon as the fresh horses appeared in the yard, my sister would spring resolutely out, and swing herself into the carriole.

'Thanks; I am ready now. Let us be off. Good-bye.'

Yes, then they would all come running after her — the umbrella, the *en-tout-cas*, the plaids with loosened strap, the bouquet, and the book, everything would be thrown into her lap, and she would hold on to them until the next station was reached, while the station-master's honest wife stood and feebly waved the young lady's pocket-handkerchief, in a manner which could not possibly attract her attention.

Although she thus lost no time, the drive was, nevertheless, extremely trying, and it was a great relief to my sister when she at length rattled down the hill from Gjelleboek, and saw Drammen extended below her. There were not many minutes left.

At last she was down in the town. 'In Drammen, in Drammen!' muttered my sister, beginning to triumph. Like a fire-engine she dashed along the streets to the station. Everything was paid. She had only to jump out of the carriole; but when she looked up at the station clock, the minute-hand was just passing the number twelve.

Undismayed, my sister collected her knick-knacks and rushed into the waiting-room, which was quite empty. But the young man who had sold the tickets, and who was in the act of drawing down the panel, caught a glimpse of this belated lady, and was good-natured enough to wait.

'A ticket — for Heaven's sake! A ticket for Drammen! What does it cost?'

'Where are you going, miss?' asked the good-natured young man.

'To Drammen—do you hear? But do make haste. I am sure the train will be gone.'

'But, miss,' said the young man, with a modest smile, 'you *are* in Drammen.'

'Ah! I beg your pardon. Yes, so I am; it is to Modum, to Modum that I want to go.'

She received her ticket, filled her lap with her things, and, purse in mouth, hurried out upon the platform.

She was instantly seized by powerful hands, lifted off the ground, and tenderly deposited in a *coupé*.

'Puff,' said the locomotive impatiently, beginning to strain at the carriages.

My sister leant back on the velvet sofa, happy and triumphant; she had been in time. Before her, upon the other sofa, she had all her dear little things, which seemed to lie and smile at her—the bouquet and the book, the *en-tout-cas* and the umbrella, and the very plaids, with the strap completely unfastened.

Then, as the train slowly began to glide out of the station, she heard the footstep of a man—rap, rap—of a man running—rap, rap, rap—running on the platform alongside the train; and although, of course, it did not concern her, still she would see what he was running for.

But no sooner did my sister's head become visible than the running man waved his arms and cried:

'There she is, there she is—the young lady who came last! Where shall we send your luggage?'

Then my sister cried in a loud and firm voice:

'To Drammen!'

And with these words she was whirled away.

LETTERS FROM MASTER-PILOT SEEHUS.

KRYDSVIG FARM,

January 1, 1889.

MR. EDITOR,

Referring to our talk of last December, when I said I was not un-willing to send you occasional letters, if anything important should happen, I do not know of anything that I could think worthy of being published or made public in your paper except the weather, which always and ever gives cause for alternate praise and blame, when one is living, so to speak, out among the sea's breakers, where there is no quietness to expect on a winter's day, but storms and rough weather as we had in the last Yule-nights, with a violent storm from the east and with such tremendous gusts of wind that the pots and pans flew about like birds. And there is much damage done by the east wind and nothing gained, because it only drives wreckage out to sea. But it was not quite so bad as it was in the great storms in the last days of November, which culminated or reached their highest point on Monday, the 26th November, when it was rougher than old folk can remember it to have ever been, with such a tremendous sea that it seemed as if it would reach the fields that we here at Krydsvig have owned from old times; it almost touched the cowhouses. After that time we had light frosts with changeable weather and a smoother sea, which was not covered, but richly sown, with many sad relics of the storm, mostly deck cargo, which is not so great a loss, as it is always lying, so to speak, upon expectancy or adventure; and when it goes, it is a relief to the ship and a great and especial blessing to these treeless coasts, par-ticularly when it comes ashore well split up and distributed, a few planks at each place, so that the Lensmand [Footnote: Sheriff's of-ficer.] cannot see any greater accumulation at any one place than that he can, with a good conscience, abandon an auction and let the folk keep what they have been lucky enough to find or diligent enough to garner in from the sea in their boats; but this time it did not repay the trouble, because of frost and an easterly land-wind, which kept the wreck from land for some time. But now the most of it has come in that is to come at this time, and it may be long to another time, as we must hope, for the seaman's sake, although I, for my part, have never been able to join with any particular devotion in prayers and supplications that we may be free from storms and foul weather; for our Lord has made the sea thus and not otherwise, so that there must come storms and tumults in the atmosphere of the air, and, as a consequence, towering billows. And it seems to me, further, that we cannot decently turn to the Lord and ask Him to do something over again or in a different way; but we can well wish each other God's help and all good luck in danger, and especially good gear for our own ones, who sail with wit and canniness, while the Englishman is mostly a demon to sail and go with full steam on in fogs and driving rain-storms, of which we can expect enough in Januarius month at the beginning of the new year, which I hope may be a good year for these coasts, with decent weather, as it may fall out, and something respectable in the way of wreckage.

Yours very truly,

LAURITZ BOLDEMANN SEEHUS,

Late Master-Pilot.

KRYDSVIG,

January 22, 1889.

MR. EDITOR,

I take up my pen to-day to inform you that I, the undersigned, address you for the last time, as I will not write more because of my sore eyes, which are not to be wondered at, after all that they have seen in bitter weather and in a long life of trouble and hardship from my youth up, mostly at sea in spray and driving snow-storms at the fishing, which is all over and past, as everything old is past. But things new are coming to the front, and here I sit alone like Job, though he, to be sure, had some friends, but loneliness is a sore thing for old folk, and idleness which they are not used to, so that the Sheriff might as well have given me back my post as master-pilot on my return from America. But he would not do it, because I was not cunning enough to agree with him, when he did not understand anybody, but it is given out officially that I am too old, and thus I sit here without having shaved for a week, because I am angry and my hand trembles, but not owing to old age. And I don't think, either, that anybody is much to be envied for having friends like Job's, and I am not stricken with boils and sitting among potsherds, but am quite hale and strong, if I am rather dried-up and stiff, but I would undertake to dance a reel and a Hamburg schottische if I could only get a girl with a fairly round waist to take hold of, but it seems to me that they are shrinking in and becoming flatter than they were in my young days; but then I think that it is surely the sore eyes that are cheating me, for I have always held this belief, that girls are girls in all times, but old folks should be quiet and mind what they understand, which is nothing that relates to the young. But a man should not get sour *in finem*, for all that, and I have found that it is a dangerous thing to grow old, for this reason, that one becomes so surly before one's time, and that is against my inner construction, and I have now sat here awhile and gazed out on the sea through rain and mist, and then I straightened my old back and spat out my quid, which in all truth smacked more of the brass box than of tobacco, because it had been chewed several times, but I have cut myself a new one with my knife, as I can no longer bite it off, for the reason that there are hardly any teeth, but I have still a few front ones, and I have one good tooth, which is hidden and is no ornament, but it is useful when I eat tough things like dried ham. And I take up the pen again because I want to let you know that I am not so ill but that I may hold out for a while yet; and, if I keep my health, you shall hear from me soon, but I have nothing to say about the weather, because we have not had any weather for a long time, and I am wondering whether this winter will come to anything, or if it will pass over in damp and wet and loose wind.

Yours very truly,

LAURITZ BOLDEMANN SEEHUS,

Late Master-Pilot.

KRYDSVIG,

April 13, 1889.

MR. EDITOR,

About the rotten feet on the sheep, which animal I by nature despise, on account of its cowardice and a tremendous silliness, the one running after the other, but if a man *will* plague himself with farming who has been a sailor from his mother's apron-string, he must keep these beasts and others like his neighbours, although he understands nothing, or very little, about the whole tribe. So I have upon my small patch of ground two good ewes, with little wit, but wool, and I sent them long before Yule to a ram at Börevig, one of the fine kind from Scotland, as folk bothered me that I must do it, because of the breed and the wool and many things, but not a rotten foot did I hear of until after much jangling among folk and a great to-do among the learned and such like, which is nothing new to me in that kind of folk, who always and always stand behind each other's backs, crying with a loud cry, 'It was not my fault,' but, faith, it was. So I say to myself, 'What shall I do with these rotten feet from Scotland, if I get the disease ingrafted, and likewise upon the innocent offspring,' who are already toddling about all three, because there were two in the one ewe. But foreign sickness is not a thing to be afflicted with, at a time when we have scab among our sheep and much else, and more than I know of, and thus I turned my look again and again to that Government, to see if it will ever gather sense. But yet the Government had not so very rotten feet in that other important matter of a Sheriff, whom we got with unexpected smartness and promptness, much to our gain and the reverse, when we think of what the man now is, but there must be a skipper all the same. And now it is growing light all over the world; that is, in our hemisphere, for spring has come upon us with extraordinary quickness, and the ice, it went with Peder-Varmestol, [Footnote: February 22nd.] and the lapwing, she came one morning with her back shining as if she had been polished out of bronze, with her crest erect, and throwing herself about in the air like a dolphin in the sea, with

74

her head down and her tail up, crying and screaming. But the lark is really the silliest creature, to sing on without ceasing the livelong day, and the sea-pie has come, and stands bobbing upon the same stone as last year, and the wild-goose and the water-wagtail. So we are all cheered up again, all the men of Jæderen, and the cod bites, too, for those who have time, but folk are mostly carting sea-weed, and ploughing and sowing, not without grumbling in some places, but the work must be done.

Yours very truly,

L.B. SEEHUS.

KRYDSVIG,

July 1, 1889.

MR. EDITOR,

Your letter of the 20th ult. received, and contents noted, and I now beg to reply that it is not very convenient, for the reason that old folk's talk is mostly about winter storms and seldom about summer, when the sun shines, and the lambs frisk and throw their tails high in the air. But, you see, they were tups all three, which was not unlooked-for after such a ram, and consequently no letter can be expected from me before autumn, when the sea gets some life in it and a grown man's voice, so to speak, for now it lies — God bless me — like a basin of milk, to the inward vexation of folk who know what the sea should be in Nature's household with ships and storms and wreckage, and a decent number of wrecks at those places where the structure of the coast permits the rescue of men and a distribution of the wreck if it be of wood, but some trash are now of iron. And I am now as parched in the hide as I was that time in Naples when the helmsman sailed the brig on to the pier-head because a hurricane had risen, and Skipper Worse and I stood on the quay and cried, though he swore mostly, and I had a basket on my arm with something that they called bananas, which they fry in butter. And it is not very nice nowadays, when the sun rises and sets in nothing but blue sky, and not a cloud to be seen, as if it were the Mediterranean of my young days, and I smell the bananas, but we here have no other stinking stuff, that I know, than ware and cods' heads. But, Mr. Editor, the young are dull and heavy with the sunshine; I myself went about singing, and wanted to show the flabby wenches of Varhaug how one once danced a real *molinask*, as it was Sunday and the young folk hung round the walls like half-dead flies in the heat. But there had been grease burnt, which made it more slippery than soft soap on the deck, and there lay the whole master-pilot in the middle of the *molinask*, and bit off the stalk of his clay pipe, but he kept his tooth, which has already been spoken about, and to his shame had to be lifted by four firm-handed fellows with much laughing, wherefore I have sat myself down in my chair to wait for the autumn, because I cannot speak or write about the drought, but only get angry and unreasonable.

Yours very truly,

LAURITZ BOLDEMANN SEEHUS.

KRYDSVIG,

October 20, 1889.

MR. EDITOR,

I could have continued my silence a very long time yet, for it has not been a great autumn either on land or sea, but little summer storms, as if for frolic, with small seas and loose wreckage, but unusually far out, about three miles from land. But the long, dark lamp-lit evenings are come, and this shoal of fish which I must write to you about and ask what the end is going to be; for now we almost think that the sea up north Stavanger way must be choke-full, as it was of herrings in the good old days that are no more, but it is now big with coal-fish, mostly north by the Reef, they say, but the undersigned and old Velas, who is a still older man, got about four boxes of right nice coal-fish yesterday, a little to the south-east. But half Jæren [Footnote: Jæderen, the coast district near Stavanger.] was on the sea, boat upon boat, for the double reason of the coal-fish and that they had not an earthly thing to do upon the land, for this year the earth has yielded us everything well and very early, but the straw is short, which, if the truth must be told, is the only thing to complain of. But the farmers are making wry faces, like the merchants in Östersöen when they complain of the herrings, for they must always complain, except about the sheep, which are going off very well to the Englishman, and I can't conceive what there will be left of this kind of beast in Jæren, but it is all the same to me, seeing that I have never liked the sheep at all until last year, when he paid taxes for all Jæren, which was more than was expected of him. And it would be well if any one were able to put bounds upon this burning of sea-ware, which the devil or somebody has invented for use as a medicine in Bergen—they say, but I do not believe it, because it has a stink that goes into the innermost part of your nostrils and into your tobacco besides. But then the east wind is good for something, at least, for it sends the heaps of ware out to sea, and I can imagine how it will surprise the Queen of England when she knows how we stink. And I have a grievance of my own, viz., boys shooting with blunderbusses and powder, and with so little wit that my eyes flash with anger every time I see them creeping on their stomachs towards a starling or a couple of lean ring-plovers, and I shout and cast stones to warn the innocent creatures, since the farmer of Jæren is, as it were, his thrall's thrall, and lets the servant-boys make a fool of him and play the concertina all night, which might be put up with, but no powder and shooting should be allowed, so that Jæren may not become a desert for bird-life, and only concertinas left and rascals of boys on their stomachs as above.

Yours very truly,

LAURITZ BOLDEMANN SEEHUS.

KRYDSVIG,

December 25, 1889.

MR. EDITOR,

After having, in the course of a long and very stormy life, given heed to the clouds of the sky and the various aspects of the sea, which can change before your eyes as you look, like a woman who discovers another whom she likes better, and you stand forsaken and rejected, because a girl's mind is like the ocean above-mentioned, and full of storms as the Spanish Sea, and I early received my shock of that kind for life, of which I do not intend to speak, but the weather is of a nature that I have never before observed in this country, with small seas, rare and moderate storms, and on this first Yule-day a peace on the earth and such a complacent calm on the sea that you might row out in a trough. The wreckage that came in on the 8th and 9th December last was the only extravagance, so to speak, of the sea this year, for there was too much in some places, and this will probably give the Lensmand a pretext for holding an auction, to the great ruination of the people, for the planks were rare ones, both long and good-hearted timber. But at an auction half the pleasure is lost, besides more that is very various in kind — for instance, brandy: and the town gentlemen who sell such liquor to the farmer must answer to their consciences what substances and ingredients such a drink is cooked out of, as it brings on mental weakness and bodily torment, proof of which I have seen numberless times in strong and well-fabricated persons, especially during the Yule-days. But this is not my friendship's time, for they say at the farm that the Oldermand [Footnote: Master-pilot] is haughty, and will not swallow their devil's drink at any price. But I sit alone before a bottle of old Jamaica, which is part of what Jacob Worse brought home from the West Indies in 1825, and I think of him and Randulf and the old ones, and the smell of the liquor seems to call up living conversations, which you can hear, and you must laugh, although you are alone, and you have such a desire to write everything down as it happened; but no more to the newspapers for this reason, that they have been after me with false teeth and a nice, neat widow, of whom nothing more will be said. And this extraordinarily mild winter has in some way kept the rheumatism out of my limbs; besides, I am strong by nature and no age to speak of; but, of course, it must be admitted that youth is better and more lively, of which, as above, nothing more will be said.

As the years go on, Mr. Editor, disappointments bite fast into us, like barnacles and mussels under ships; but we ourselves do not feel that our speed is decreasing, and that we are dropping astern, and, as already hinted, old age does not protect us against folly.

Yours very truly,

OLD DANCES.

We really strove honestly, swung ourselves and swung our ladies, although many were stiff enough to get round. We were not invited to a ball; this dance was merely a surprise frolic.

We had dined in all good faith — at least, the stranger cousin had; and while I stood thinking of coffee, and dreading no danger, the house began to swarm with young folks who had dined upstairs or downstairs, or at home, or not at all, or God knows where. The dining-room doors were thrown open again, the floor was cleared as if by magic, partners caught hold of each other, two rushed to the piano, and — one, two, three, they were in the middle of a galop before I could recover my wits.

They immediately forsook me again, when I received a frightful blow in the region of the heart. It was Uncle Ivar himself, who shouted:

'Come, boy; inside with you, and move your legs. Don't stand there like a snivelling chamberlain, but show what kind of fellow you are with those long pipe-stalks that our Lord has sent you out upon.'

Thus the dance began; and although I did not at all like uncle's way of arranging matters, I good-naturedly set to work, and we strove honestly, that I can say, with the cousins as well as the lighter of the aunts.

By degrees we even became lively; and everything might have passed off in peace and joy if uncle had not taken it into his head that we were not doing our utmost in the dance, especially we gentlemen.

'What kind of dancing is that to show to people?' he exclaimed contemptuously. 'There they go, mincing and tripping, as spindle-shanked as pencils and parasols. No, there was another kind of legs in my time! Pooh, boys, that was dancing, that was!'

We held up our heads and footed it until our ears tingled. But every time that Uncle Ivar passed the ball-room door, his jeers became more aggravating, until we were almost exhausted, each one trying to be nimbler than another.

But what was the use? Every time uncle came back from his round through the smoking-room, where he cooled his head in an enormous ale-bowl, he was bolder and bolder, and at last he had aled so long in the cooling bowl that his boldness was not to be repressed.

'Out of the way with these long-shanked flamingoes!' he cried. 'Now, boys, you are going to see a real national dance. Come, Aunt Knoph, we two old ones will make these miserable youngsters of nowadays think shame.'

'Oh, no, my dear, do let me alone,' begged respectable Mrs. Knoph; 'remember, we are both old.'

'The devil is old,' laughed uncle merrily; 'you were the smartest of the lasses, and I was not the greatest lout among the boys, that I know. So come along, old girl!'

'Oh no, my dear Ivaren; won't you excuse me?' pleaded Mrs. Knoph. But what was the use? The hall was cleared, room had to be made, and we miserable flamingoes were squeezed up against the walls, so that we might be out of the way, at all events.

All the young ladies were annoyed at the interruption, and we gentlemen were more or less sulky over all the affronts that we had endured. But the lady who had to play was quite in despair. She had merely received orders to play something purely national; and no matter how often she asked what dance it was to be, uncle would only stare politely at her over his spectacles, and swear that this would be another kind of dance.

As far as Uncle Ivar was concerned, 'Sons of Norway' was no doubt good enough for any or every dance; and as to the dance itself, the music was really not so very important; for, you see, it happened in this way:

Uncle Ivar came swinging in with one arm by his side, and tall, respectable Mrs. Knoph on the other. He placed her with a chivalrous sweep in the middle of the floor, bowed in the fashion of elderly gallants, with head down between his legs and arms hanging in front, but quickly straightened himself up again and looked about with a provoking smile.

Uncle Ivar, without a coat and with vest unbuttoned, was a sight to see in a ball-room. A flaming red poll, one of the points of his collar up and one down, his false shirtfront thrust under a pair of home-made braces, which were green, two white bands of tape hanging down, a tuft of woollen shirt visible here and there.

But one began to respect the braces when one saw what they carried—a trousers-button as big as a square-sail, and another behind—I am sure that one could have written 'Constantinople' in full across it in a large hand.

'Tush, boys!' cried uncle, clapping his hands, 'now, by Jove, you shall see a dance worth looking at!' And then it began—at least, I *think* that it began here, but, as will presently appear, this is not quite certain. It happened in this way:

The pianist struck up some national tune or other; uncle swung his arms and shuffled a little with his feet, amorously ogling old Mrs. Knoph over his spectacles.

All attention was now concentrated upon Uncle Ivar's legs; it was clear that after the little preliminary steps he would let himself go! I stood and wondered whether he would spring into the air clear over Mrs. Knoph, or only kick the cap off her head.

That would have been quite like him, and it is not at all certain whether he himself did not think of performing some such feat, for, as will presently appear, we cannot know; it happened, you see, in this way:

As Uncle Ivar, after some little pattering, collected his energies for the decisive *coup*, he violently stamped his feet upon the floor.

But, as if he had trodden upon soft soap, like lightning his heels glided forward from under him. The whole of Uncle Ivar fell backward upon Constantinople, his legs beat the air, and the crown of his head struck the floor with a boom that resounded through the whole house.

Yes, there he lay stretched in all his *rondeur*, with the square-sail just in front of the feet of respectable Mrs. Knoph, who resembled a deserted tower in the desert.

I was irreverent enough to let the others gather him up. Of course he would not fall to pieces; I knew the Constantinople architecture. I slipped out into the corridor and laughed until I was quite exhausted.

But since then I have often wondered what kind of dance it could have been.

AUTUMN.

AARRE,

October 7, 1890.

I had intended to send a few observations upon the wild-goose to *Nature,* but since they have extended to quite a long letter, they go to *Dagbladet.* It is not because I believe that they represent anything new that no one has observed before; but I know how thoughtlessly most of us let the sun shine, and the birds fly, without any idea of what a refreshment it is for a man's soul to understand what he sees in Nature, and how interesting animal life becomes when we have once learned that there is a method and a thought in every single thing that the animal undertakes, and what a pleasure it is to discover this thought, and trace the beautiful reasoning power which is Nature's essence.

And thus most of us go through life, and down into a hole in the ground like moles, without having taken any notice of the bird that flew or the bill that sang. We believe that the small birds are sparrows, the larger probably crows; barndoor fowls are the only ones we know definitely.

I met a lady the other day who was extremely indignant about this. She had asked the man at whose house she was staying—a very intelligent peasant—what kind of bird it was that she had seen in the fields. It was evident that it was a thrush—merely a common thrush—and she described the bird to him: it was about half as large as a pigeon, gray and speckled with yellow; it hopped in the fields, and so on.

'Would it be the bird they call a swallow?' suggested the man.

'Not at all,' replied the lady angrily. 'I rather think it was a kind of thrush.'

'Oh! then you had better ask my wife.'

'So she understands birds, does she?' exclaimed the lady, much mollified.

'Yes, she is mad with them, they do so much mischief among the cherries.'

With this my lady had to go. But the story is not yet finished; the worst is to come.

For when, indignant at the countryman's ignorance of the bird-world, she told all this in town, there was one very solemn gentleman who said:

'Are you sure that it was not a gull?'

This went beyond all bounds, thought my lady, and she came and complained bitterly to me.

When wild-geese fly in good order, as they do when in the air for days and nights together, the lines generally form the well-known plough, with one bird at the point, and the two next ones on either side of him a little way behind.

Hitherto I have always been content with the explanation that we received and gave one another as boys, viz., that the birds chose this formation in order to cleave the air, like a snow-plough clearing a way.

But it suddenly occurred to me the other day that this was pure nonsense — an association of ideas called forth by the resemblance to a plough, which moves in earth or snow, but which has no meaning up in the air.

What *is* cloven air? And who gets any benefit by it?

Yes, if the geese flew as they walk — one directly behind the other — there might perhaps, in a contrary wind, be some little shelter and relief for the very last ones. But they fly nearly side by side in such a manner that each one, from first to last, receives completely 'uncloven' air right in the breast; there can be no suggestion that it is easier for the last than for the first bird to cut a way.

The peculiar order of flight has quite another meaning, viz., to keep the flock together on the long and fatiguing journey; and if we start from this basis, the reasoning thought becomes also evident in the arrangement itself.

Out here by the broad Aarre Water there pass great flights of wild-geese; and in bad weather it may happen that they sit in thousands on the water, resting and waiting.

But even if the flock flies past, there is always uneasiness and noise when they come over Aarre Water. The ranks break, for a time the whole becomes a confused mass, while they all scream and quack at the same time.

Only slowly do they form again and fly southward in long lines, until they shrink to thinner and thinner threads in the gray autumn sky, and their last sound follows them upon the north wind.

Then I always believe that there has been a debate as to whether they should take a little rest down on Aarre Water. There are certainly many old ones who know the place again, and plenty of the young are tender-winged, and would fain sit on the water and dawdle away a half-day's time.

But when it is eventually resolved to fly on without stopping, and the lines again begin to arrange themselves, it has become clear to me that each seeks his own place in the ranks slanting outwards behind the leaders, so that by this means he may be conducted along with the train without being under the necessity of troubling about the way.

If these large, heavy birds were to fly in a cluster for weeks, day and night, separation and confusion would be inevitable. They would get in each other's way every minute with their heavy wings, there would be such a noise that the leader's voice could not be distinguished, and it would be impossible to keep an eye upon him after dark. Besides, over half the number are young birds, who are undertaking this tremendous journey for the first time, and who naturally, at Aarre Water, begin to ask if it be the Nile that they see. Time would be lost, the flock would be broken up, and all the young would perish on the journey, if there were not, in the very disposition of the ranks, something of the beautiful reasoning thought binding them together.

Let us now consider the first bird, who leads the flock— presumably an old experienced gander. He feels an impulse towards the south, but he undoubtedly bends his neck and looks down for known marks in the landscape. That is why the great flocks of geese follow our coast-line southward until the land is lost to view.

But the birds do not look straight forward in the direction of their bills: they look to both sides. Therefore, the bird next to the leader does not follow right behind him in the 'cloven' air, but flies nearly alongside, so that it has the leader in a direct line with its right or left eye at a distance of about two wing-flaps.

And the next bird does the same, and the next; each keeps at the same distance from its fore-bird.

And what each bird sees of its fore-bird are the very whitest feathers of the whole goose, under the wings and towards the tail, and this, in dark nights, is of great assistance to the tired, half-sleeping creatures.

Thus each, except the pilot himself, has a fore-bird's white body in a line with one eye, and more they do not need to trouble about. They can put all their strength into the monotonous work of wing-flapping, as long as they merely keep the one eye half open and see that they have the fore-bird in his place. Thus they know that all is in order, that they are in connection with the train, and with him at the head who knows the way.

If from any cause a disturbance arises, it is soon arranged upon this principle; and when the geese have flown a day or two from the starting-point, such rearrangement is doubtless effected more rapidly and more easily. For I am convinced that they soon come to know one another personally so well that each at once finds his comrade in flight, whom he is accustomed to have before his eye, and therefore they are able to take their fixed places in the ranks as surely and accurately as trained soldiers.

We can all the more readily imagine such a personal acquaintance among animals, as we know that even men learn with comparative ease to distinguish individuals in flocks of the same species of beasts. If we townspeople see a flock of sheep, it presents to us the same ovine face — only with some difference between old and young. But a peasant-woman can at once take out her two or three ewes from the big flock that stands staring by the door — indeed, she can even recognise very young lambs by their faces.

Thus I believe I understand the reason for the wild-goose's order of flight better than when I thought of a plough that 'clove' the air; and, as already stated, it may well be that many have been just as wise long ago. But I venture to wager that the great majority of people have never thought of the matter at all, and I fear that multitudes will think of it somewhat in this fashion: 'What is it to me how those silly geese fly?'

I often revert to the strangely thoughtless manner in which knowledge of animal life is skipped over in the teaching of the young. The rude and wild conception of animals which the clergy teach from the Old Testament seems to cause only deep indifference on the part of the girls, and, in the boys, an unholy desire to ramble about and blaze away with a gun.

Here there has been a shooting as on a drill-ground all the summer, until now only the necessary domestic animals are left. Among the cows, the starlings were shot into tatters, so that they crawled wingless, legless, maimed, into holes in the stone fences to die. If a respectable curlew sat by the water's edge mirroring his long bill, a rascal of a hunter lay behind a stone and sighted; and was there a water-puddle with rushes that could conceal a young duck, there immediately came a fully-armed hero with raised gun. Even English have been here! They had some new kind of guns—people said—that shot as far as you pleased, and round corners and behind knolls. They murdered, I assure you; they laid the district bare as pest and pox! I must stop, for I am growing so angry.

I have had thoughts of applying for a post as inspector of birds in the Westland. I should travel round and teach people about the birds, exhibit the common ones, so that all might have the pleasure of recognising them in Nature; accustom people to listen to their song and cry, and to take an interest in their life, their nests, eggs, and young.

Then I should inflame the peasants against the armed farm-boys, day-labourers, and poachers, and against the sportsmen from town, who stroll around without permission and crack away where they please. It only wants a beginning and a little combination, for the peasant, in his heart, is furious at this senseless shooting.

Perhaps some day, when not a single bird is left, my idea of an in-spector may come to be honoured and valued. Would that a godly Storthing [Footnote: Parliament.] may then succeed in finding a pious and well-recommended man, who can instruct the people in a moral manner as to where the humid Noah accommodated the ostriches in the ark, or what he managed to teach the parrots during the prolonged rainy weather.

We, too, have recently had a deluge. The lakes and the river have risen to the highest winter-marks. But the soil of this blessed place is so sandy that roads and fields remain firm and dry, the water run-ning off and disappearing in a moment.

It has also blown from all quarters, with varying force, for three weeks. We press onward over the plain, and stagger about among the houses, where the gusts of wind rush in quite unexpectedly with loud claps. The fishing-rod has had to be carried against the wind, and the water of the river has risen in the air like smoke.

And the sea, white with wrath, begins to form great heavy break-ers far out in many fathoms of water, rolls them in upon the strand, inundates large tracts, and carries away the young wrack-grass and what we call 'strandkaal' [Footnote: Sea-kale.]—all that has grown in summer and gathered a little flying sand around it as tiny fortifications; the sea has washed the beach quite bare again, and fixed its old limits high up among the sand-heaps, where they are strong enough to hold out for the winter.

I have now been here four months to a day, and have seen the corn since it was light-green shoots until now, when it is well secured in the barns,—where there was room. For the crop has been so heavy—not in the memory of man has there been such a year on this coast—that rich stacks of corn are standing on many farms, and the lofts are crammed to the roof-trees.

Inland there is corn yet standing out; it is yellowing on the fields, which are here green and fresh as in the middle of spring.

We have had many fine days; but autumn is the time when Jæderen is seen at its best.

As the landscape nowhere rises to any great height, we always see much sky; and, although we do not really know it, we look quite as much at the magnificent, changeful clouds as at the fine scenery, which recedes far into the distance and is never strikingly prominent.

And all day long, in storm and violent showers, the autumn sky changes, as if in a passionate uproar of wrath and threatenings, alternating with reconciliation and promise, with dark brewing storm-clouds, gleams of sunshine and rainbows, until the evening, when all is gathered together out on the sea to the west.

Then cloud chases cloud, with deep openings between, which shine with a lurid yellow. The great bubbling storm-clouds form a framework around the western sky, while everywhere shoot yellow streaks and red beams, which die away and disappear and are pressed down into the sea, until we see only one sickly yellow stripe of light, far out upon the wave.

Then darkness rolls up from the sea in the west and glides down from the fjelds in the east, lays itself to rest upon the black wastes of heather, and spreads an uncanny covering over the troubled Aarre Waters, which groan and sob and sigh among rushes and stones. A stupendous melancholy rises up from the sea and overflows all things, while the wakeful breakers, ever faithful, murmur their watchman-song the livelong night.